DARWIN WAS NOT THERE
ON THAT DAY

A Different History Of Creation

NEW EDITION

GERALD PATRICK CURRAN

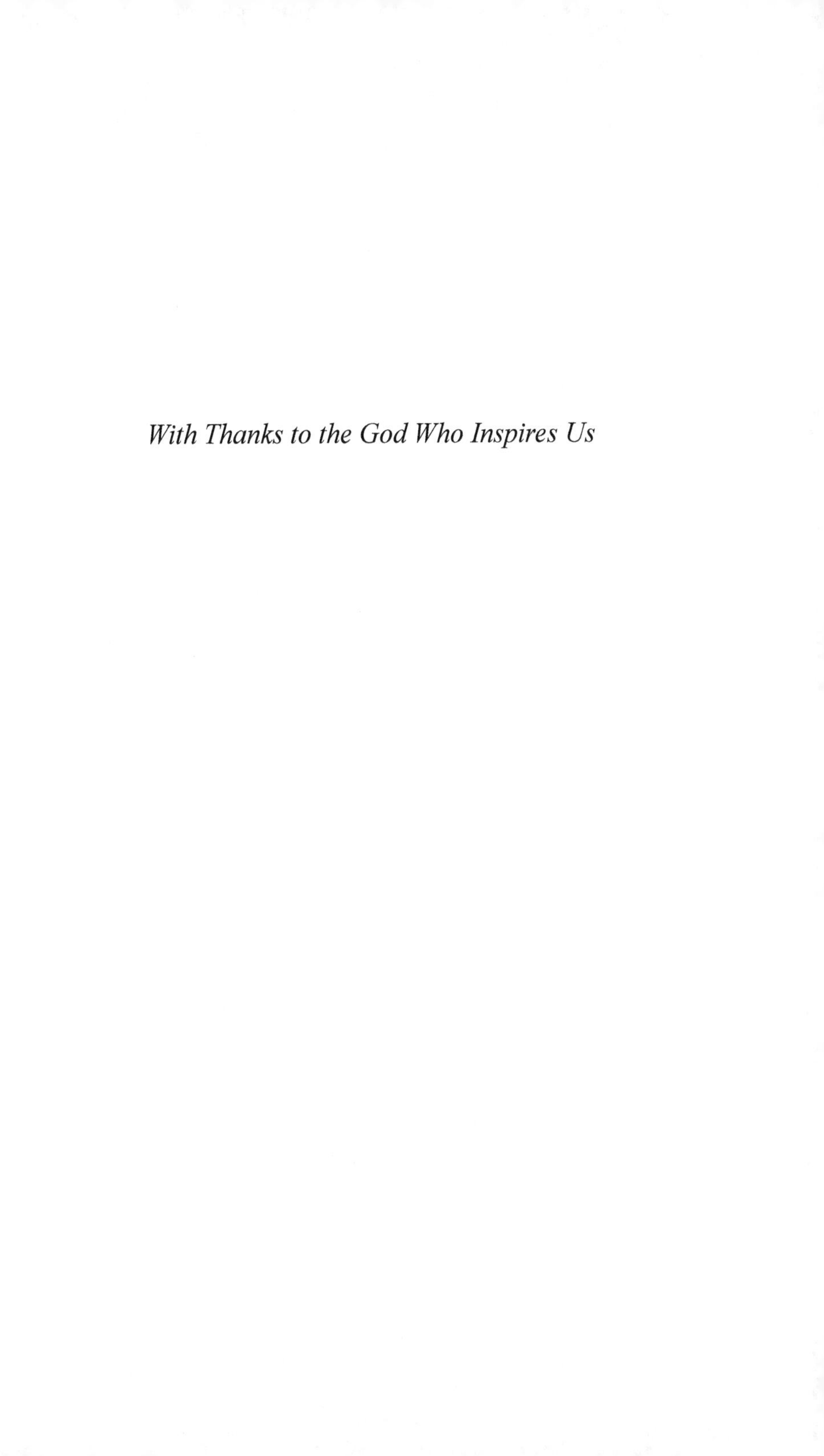

With Thanks to the God Who Inspires Us

PROLOGUE

For generations, scientists have struggled with ideas about our origins. They developed many theories such as Evolution, Natural Selection, an infinitely expanding Universe. The Reverend Georges Lemaitre, of Belgium, brought us his theory of the beginning of the Universe. This is sometimes called the Big Bang theory. Rebecca L. Cann, a geneticist based in Los Angeles, brought us the possible identity of our first mother. Both theories invite us to think in new ways about our world. We may be reminded of them as we journey through the adventures found in the chapters of this book.

1

NEWS FROM SPACE

"There have been some deaths in an accident on Mars…"

The word Mars got McAlister's attention as he listened to the morning news. Alex McAlister was just heading out to work. He stopped just outside the kitchen and listened to the rest of the news report.

"Are you coming with me Alisa? I'm just about ready to leave," he called his daughter.

"Oh, coming, Daddy. I'm just putting on my shoes. … No Scottie, not today. We're just going to Daddy's work."

The dog whimpered a little as Alisa closed the apartment door behind her. Father and daughter walked to the Elcrocar on the Charging Rack. When they had slid into their seats, they headed for Glasgow.

When they had reached the university and the Elcrocar was stacked on a trestle, they headed straight for the laboratory. Alisa was on school holidays, and this was one of the quiet days when she could come with her father. Though a little girl she liked being with her Daddy watching what he was doing. For his part, he just had to be careful that she was safe. She was mostly happy just to sit beside him on a high chair.

Ali Hasan was already in the lab at the radiation booth.

"…Morning Ali. Alisa this is Sayyed Hasan. We are both working on the same project. Ali, this is my daughter, Alisa, she will be with me today, school holidays you know."

"Pleased to meet you, Miss Alisa. Just be careful in here; some areas are dangerous."

"Saba al-khayer, Sade."

"Oh, you speak Arabic Alisa?"

"Well yes, we learn Arabic at school."

"That's nice. Your pronunciation is very good."

The research project involved experiments to find a mostly primitive technology that will produce oxygen molecules from Mars's basalt rock. The process would be used by teams undertaking exploration of the red planet.

They had failed in the race to be the first lab to produce molybdenum fibers from the chemicals available on Mars. A lab in the Islamic Confederation had first achieved that feat. If their lab at the University of Glasgow achieved a breakthrough, they would get back in the news; at least that's what Alex McAlister thought. On his worktop were ray emitters, electronic gauges, glass tubes, and lumps of reddish rock.

Alisa stretched out her hand and pointed, "What is that, Daddy?"

"Well, it's not too complicated. We're trying to use basic chemistry to see if we can make these rocks super-

produce large amounts of oxygen. It's like some of the things you do in House Science class in school."

"I don't have House Science until next year."

"Oh well, it's basically what happens in Mom's kitchen. If I ever go to work on Mars, I would be doing the same thing there, helping the settlement project produce much more oxygen."

"But Daddy, why would you have to go? You know how lonely it would be without you."

"Well, we shall see Alisa. Meanwhile, I just have to check some results here. Are you comfortable?"

"I'm fine, Daddy."

"We can go to the Gharfa café for a break at ten."

2

MARCHING ORDERS

McAlister sat at his station in the laboratory throughout that day. But he had difficulty concentrating on the research. His mind kept drifting back to the morning news about Mars. He wondered whether his application to work there would now go through. He thought, 'It must go through now. My experience in materials testing should seal the deal.'

Alex McAlister had never fully understood why he had chosen astrophysics as a career, although he had engineering in his blood. Two of his uncles had been aeronautical engineers.

He remembered one saying, "…I've been so blessed; I've been able to use my gifts for the good of humanity…"

He realized early on in his studies that the Mars Settlement Project would loom large in his life. He had thought, 'Perhaps I inherited a spark for service from my ancestors.'

When he felt a glow from his Tabnax, he had a hunch about what a new message might be.

It said, "We are pleased to inform you that as of 11:35 hours today, June 25th. 2098, applicant Alexander N. McAlister has been accepted for the position of Auxiliary Team Engineer for the Mars Settlement Project. Alexander N. McAlister must complete the registration details and report to the Commander at Pondicherry Space Service Center by 13:00 hours on July 20th 2098 at the latest. He will complete his project orientation at that time."

McAlister paused for a moment and thought, 'I will not tell Alisa anything about this until I tell Janet.'

When father and daughter went out to the Elcrocar that evening, instead of heading for the gym McAlister decided to drive to Coats Observatory Museum. He would like to take a sentimental look at Mars through the old telescope. This was the telescope through which he first saw Mars as a boy. Alisa would love to have a peek too, but he would not be telling her his news. She knew that he had applied for the job but hoped against hope that he would never leave Paisley Old Town.

As they drove this way, he always had a disturbing memory whenever he passed by East Lane. He would remember the times, as he cycled by St. Timothy's Klassika School when the Roman Catholic boys would throw stones and shout nicknames.

As an adult, some of the apprehension was still there. He sometimes thought, 'Did religion have something to do with kids throwing rocks? What kind of faith is that? I hope there won't be any Roman Catholics on Mars.' Driving further on he thought, 'Anyway, those people are always too carefree and unserious.'

When they got to the Coats Observatory Museum, old Sayyed Mahmood was on duty.

"Well, good evening, Miss Alisa. You've brought your Dad along today. How are you, Mister McAlister? Haven't seen you for a while."

"I'm here just for old times' sake. Is the old telescope available? I'd like to have a peek. The first time I looked at Mars was through old Spikey. You know, I used to come to the talks here every week. I have lots of good memories."

"Oh, good. Alisa, you know where the lighting controls are. Take your father up to old Spikey."

"Let's go, Daddy."

3

A SAD FAREWELL

When they had returned to their apartment at Blenheim Court, supper was ready.

McAlister waited until the meal was over before he broke the news to his wife, "Darling, I've got that position on Mars. They need me to leave next month."

"Oh, Daddy, you can't," Alisa pleaded, "Don't go."

"Well, Alex, congratulations. I know this is what you've prepared for. It is a great honor."

Alisa and Charles came around the table to hug their father.

"Don't go, Daddy. The little green men are waiting to eat you," said Charles.

"Your mom said she's proud of me and understands."

"But it's not a few months, Daddy. I asked Sayyed Mahmood, and he said that going to Mars and coming back again takes more than two years. It's too long!" said Alisa.

McAlister had known that it would be hard for his children to take, especially Alisa. He was glad to have the support of his wife.

Over the next few weeks, he made a point of spending extra time with Alisa, Charles, and Janice. On two weekends, they spent a happy day at Largs Bay Beach. One Saturday, he spent an afternoon with Alisa and Charles studying Mars with the new Electron Spectrometer Telescope. They also took a nostalgic peek through the old hand-focus telescope.

As the day approached for his departure, McAlister had hoped to have grown closer to his family. But of course, when the family climbed into the Elcrocab for the ride to Glasgow Global Drome, there was an even greater sense of sadness. Alisa had brought her teddy bear along for comfort, in anticipation of the pain of her Daddy's departure.

When they reached the Drome Transfer Concourse it was time to say goodbye. Arabic piped music was echoing through the concourse as McAlister hugged his wife and bent down to hug Alisa and Charles. As soon as he wrapped his arms around Alisa she started to cry.

"Oh, Daddy, I'm going to miss you so. I'm going to miss you so much," she sobbed, throwing her arms around his waist.

Charles got an awkward hug before his dad was able to extricate himself. When his Alamtah Bags had been transferred, Alexander N. McAlister strode to the Security Portal. Janice, Alisa, and Charles hugged each other as he disappeared.

When the trio had returned to their apartment Alisa

said, "Mum, I'm going over to the observatory. I want to see Mars."

"Be careful, darling. It's going to get cold and dark. Don't be long."

The little girl threw her teddy bear onto a chair and ran out the front door. Alisa kept running until she came to the main entrance of Coats Observatory. She hoped that Sayyed Mahmood would be the one on duty. She knew that he would let her in.

"Oh, Sayyed Mahmood, my Daddy is going away, and I feel so sad," the little girl burst out crying and threw herself onto a chair.

Mahmood left his perch at the monitors. He sat down beside the girl and said, "Young lady, what are you doing up so late in the evening? Do you know what the time is?" He continued, "You know we'll miss your dad too. He was one of the most successful of all the students who used to come here. People like you, and him, make everything worthwhile."

"It is just so unfair that he is going so far away."

"Look...come and see Mars. This is a good night to see it. It looks so beautiful on a night like this," Mahmood tried to cut through Alisa's sadness.

"No, no...I won't look. It's a horrible planet. I hate it!" Alisa rushed for the exit doors.

She stopped outside on the pavement and stood looking up at the sky. Tears again began to trickle down her cheeks.

4

ANOTHER KIND OF JOURNEY

"Greetings young lady. I am your servant Absolin."

Suddenly there, in front of Alisa, was a huge translucent ball. Inside the ball stood a tall glowing being with wings. It was the being's voice that Alisa could hear.

She was shocked and asked, "Who…who are you?"

"I am Absolin, a lesser Angel. I have been sent to help you with the great longing that you feel."

"How…how did you know?"

"Well…will you come with me so we can find the answer?"

Alisa's eyes were fixed on those of the bright being. But she had a feeling of peace and said, "What do I need to do?"

"If you will step with me into my Bubble we can go to a place of healing and refreshment."

Alisa hesitated, but the feeling of peace was so soothing. She stepped forward into the Bubble and stood beside the Angel. The Bubble began to move, and in no time, they were flying up and away from Paisley Old Town and soaring out over Glasgow. Alisa could see the outline of the River Clyde passing below.

They were traveling in the Bubble across the blackness of Space. The little girl was among the stars passing through the vastness. Peace had enveloped Alisa and the stress of the longing for her father was seeping away. She dropped down and rested her head against the Angel.

"Where are we going?" asked Alisa, "Is it far?"

"We are going to a place called Outer Paradise. It is where those who serve in Paradise go to relax and unwind. Paradise can get very intense, so Outer Paradise is there as a restful escape. There are serene gardens and parks, pools and fountains, orchards and forests, all in which to relax. There are places to join with friends and Nectar Cafes in which to enjoy an infinite number of delicious foods. After a stay in Outer Paradise any being who serves in Paradise Proper is fully refreshed, you'll see."

They had been traveling through Space and Time when Alisa was suddenly awakened. Far above, in the darkness, there appeared a row of gates that spewed out multi-colored flames. These had appeared out of the nothingness.

"What is that?" asked Alisa.

"Oh, those are the Gates of Hell. They can pop up anywhere."

Out through the flames shot dark figures. These turned and began to swoop downwards. Alisa could see that they were Demons, just like the ones in that film. They were charging straight towards the Bubble and they waved some kind of weapon. It was a frightening sight. Alisa was terrified and clung to Absolin. 'Would they puncture the

Bubble?' she thought. She hid her face and screwed up into a ball.

Just as the Demons got close, a flurry of massive Angels appeared flashing their swords. These flew between the Bubble and the Demons. The dark figures stopped in midair. They turned around and scurried back to the flames. When the last Demon had disappeared the Gates of Hell faded to nothing and the Angels flew away. Absolin and Alisa continued on their journey.

The Angel said, "Alisa, I apologize for the Demons. I didn't expect to see them at this time."

5

REACHING THE DESTINATION

ALISA STARED out of the Bubble into the vastness of space. There were no stars now but a glowing light appeared as a spot in the distance.

"I suppose it must seem like a long time to you Alisa, but we have only been traveling for a millisecond of your time. Look, we are just about at Outer Paradise now."

The glowing light grew and grew until Alisa could make out what appeared to be a shining city floating in the darkness.

"Is that where we are going?"

"This is part of Paradise, Alisa. It is called Outer Paradise. I will only be able to take you here. Paradise Proper has some special requirements for beings to be allowed to enter. It's a rule that they've had for eons. Outer Paradise is where those who serve in Paradise take a break from the intense excitement that can be part of life in Paradise Proper. There is a sense of relaxation, and they can unwind and rest for a time, in less intense surroundings. We are getting close now."

Suddenly the Bubble bounced and stopped as though it had bumped into something.

"We have bumped into the Invisible Barrier that separates this Vacuum Dimension from the atmosphere of Outer Paradise. We will have to find one of the entrances."

The Bubble moved around until Absolin said, "I see some Armored Seraphim over there. That is where we can enter."

The Bubble slid into Outer Paradise and swooped downwards past crystal battlements on both sides. Other shining Bubbles floated by as their Bubble sank further towards their destination.

"We're just about to land," said Absolin.

The Bubble dropped into the middle of a tree-lined courtyard, where it hovered a little above the ground. Alisa stepped out gingerly and looked around in awe. The air was full of a sweet perfume and choral harmonies.

"We'll head for a Nectar Café. I'm sure you are famished by the trip."

"Oh my. Yes, I am!"

"First, I'd like to get you some clothes suitable for Outer Paradise."

They stepped through an alcove at the side of the courtyard and through a doorway. There they entered a gallery filled with racks of gowns and uniforms of many colors. When Alisa was fitted with a silver tunic with a golden cord belt it was time to head for a Nectar Café.

6

AT A NECTAR CAFÉ

WALKING SIDE BY SIDE, Absolin and Alisa reached a golden archway which led to a flight of luminous steps. At the top of the steps was an orchard of fruit trees. Lines of trees seemed to disappear into the distance in every direction, except for a clearing straight ahead.

"There is a Nectar Café right over there where we can relax and where you can get something to eat and drink. Outer Paradise will be a good place for you to forget your pain and sorrow."

As they walked along, Alisa could see that the leaves and fruits above them were of different colors and sizes. The fruits all looked delicious. Ahead were glittering tables and chairs spaced in a large circle. At some of the tables sat groups of diners. Alisa noticed that some of the diners had wings. She thought, 'Those must be Angels, like Absolin.'

"Is this the Nectar Café?" asked Alisa.

"Yes Alisa. We'll find a seat and get you some nectar,"

Before they could find a table, they were surrounded by

a group of Seraphim that had just come from their Times of Worship in Paradise.

"Where have you been Absolin? …What have we got here?"

The Seraphim were immediately curious about Alisa,

"Aren't you going to introduce us?"

"Honorable Seraphim, I would like you all to meet Alisa. She, for it is a girl, has come to us from a different dimension…and a different time. She needs our love and support."

"Well, all right, we have just come from our Times of Worship. We need to relax and unwind. Why don't you come and join us at table?"

The group moved further into the Nectar Café and took their places at a big round table. Alisa was seated between Absolin and a Seraph. At first, her head was below the tabletop, but then her chair miraculously adjusted, so that she was at exactly the right height. Hovering towards them was a Cherub in a pink apron.

On reaching their table, he asked, "What kind of nectar will the Honorable Heavenly Servants be having? There is Peach Blossom Nectar, Paradise Surprise Nectar, Fruit Flavorful Nectar, and an infinite number of other nectars. I will make a guess and suggest that the stranger would like the Paradise Surprise Nectar. I know they would enjoy it."

After a pause, Alisa said, "All right, I'll try that. I just hope my tummy can handle Nectar Café food. I haven't had any before."

"Oh, your tummy will be just fine, you'll see," said Absolin.

Just then, another Cherub in a pink apron, came floating

by. He carried a silver tray laden with several sparkling tall glasses. The Cherub seemed to know beforehand what each one wanted and began to place the right nectar before each.

Alisa looked intently at the glass in front of her, "Oh, I love the glowing blossoms floating on the top. Oh my, and the golden straw."

7

THE PURPLE BEINGS

ACROSS FROM WHERE Absolin and Alisa were sitting was a table with a large group of Purple Dominions. Absolin recognized them as old friends from eons ago.

He said to Alisa, "I see some old friends of mine over there. Let's go and talk to them. I'm sure they'd like to meet you. Please excuse us Honorable Seraphim. I would like to introduce Alisa to the Purple Dominions."

Alisa climbed down from her chair to meet these strange-looking purple beings.

As they reached the other table Absolin said, "Hallo, Honorable Dominions. Welcome back to Outer Paradise. You must be thrilled for a change in pace and being able to catch up with your fellows."

"Oh, hallo Absolin," It was the closest Dominion, "Thanks for the greeting. Yes, it's wonderful to be able to catch up to our old group...amazing how we can't stop talking at a time like this."

"Honorable Dominions, I'd like to introduce you to

Alisa, my friend. She comes from a different time and dimension and will be with us for a while."

"Hallo Alisa. Welcome to Outer Paradise. Perhaps it's not the real thing, but for us, at a time like this, it's just great. Why don't you both take a seat? There's a high seat near me here, so Alisa might like to sit there," said the Dominion.

"All right, Alisa, you sit there, and I'll squeeze in beside you," said Absolin.

"So, Alisa, is this your first visit to Outer Paradise… have you been here before? Some stranger beings really like it."

Alisa's little voice began, "This is my first time. I never thought that I would ever be in such a beautiful place. It's just wonderful. I'm looking forward so much to seeing everything. Absolin says we're going to do a tour everywhere."

"So, what's a she? I've never heard that word before," it was a rather stern-looking Dominion speaking from across the table.

"What's special about a she then?" he growled the words.

"I'll explain everything," said Absolin, his wings stiffening slightly. "Alisa is a little girl, a she. At her time and in her dimension, there are two kinds of the same being. They are complementary. This means that they rely on each other in different ways. There are she's, and he's, and Alisa is a she."

"But why should there be two kinds of the same being? Shouldn't each being be enough unto itself?" he growled.

"Well, I don't know the answer to that. Perhaps the

great I Am Who I Am would know. They will both be created for Him. I can't really answer your question. I guess it's just another of those mysteries that surround us everywhere. Can you say anything, Alisa?" asked Absolin.

"Well," her little voice began, "All I know is that I've always wanted a little brother, and maybe that's because he would be different from me. But Elga, our neighbor, just got married to a man, perhaps because he's different from her. But I'm just guessing!"

The Purple Dominion threw up his hands, "So now we've got a she, a brother, and a man. I'm completely lost. Who are these creatures?"

"They all complement each other, as I said," said Absolin, "The he and the man are both one kind while a she is another kind of the same type of being. It's not all that complicated."

"Well, it confounds me," said the Dominion, "Hey, why don't you both have a nectar on me while we Purple Dominions catch up on some yarns."

"Thank you for the offer, but Alisa and I need to talk privately, by ourselves. Please excuse us. We will leave you Honorable Dominions to yourselves."

8

A TALK WITH A WISE ADVISOR

THE ANGEL and the little girl bowed toward the Purple Dominions and walked away under the trees. They walked to the edge of flowering gardens.

"Alisa, I've asked the Principality Milab to meet us here. He is very ancient and wise. Don't be put off by his color. His face is peach and his clothes are shades of peach, quite pretty, really. I would like him to meet with you so you can share your story with him."

"All right," said Alisa, "will you be there too?"

"Of course, Alisa. I will be right there. Oh, I see Milab floating towards us in the distance."

When Milab got close, he said, "Hallo Absolin. I heard your message. I would certainly love to talk to Alisa. Although I have never spoken with a girl, is that what you said they are?"

"Alisa, I would like to introduce you to the Honorable Principality Milab. Actually, we just call him Mili, isn't that right, Milab?"

"That's right, Absolin, it's my favorite name," he towered over Alisa but bent down to smile broadly.

"I'm very happy to be here," said Alisa, "I've never been in such a beautiful place."

Milab said, "Let us take a saunter through the gardens. It's very quiet after the birdsong. You don't mind if I lift you up so it's easier to talk?"

"Oh no, I think I'd like that."

"Absolin tells me that you are very sad. Now, what exactly are you sad about then?"

"Well, I'm sad because I miss my Daddy. He has gone on a transport ship to Mars, which is so far away. He will be gone for a long time. He told me that he would be learning about the planet, but why couldn't he just learn from books?" She paused, "We live near the observatory. Now I will have to go there every day to see where he is. There are telescopes and Visiscreens. These might console me a bit, but I miss him so."

"Your story really touches my spirit," said the Principality, "It sounds terrible. But tell me, what is a daddy then?"

"Well, a daddy gives you life. He is your father. You would not be alive without a daddy."

"So, accepting that this daddy father is so far away, what do you think we should do about the situation?" asked the Principality.

"I think perhaps that the only thing for me to do is to take my mind off my pain and think about pleasant things."

"Well, I think you came up with a good answer there. You have solved the problem yourself. But I will let Absolin know if I think of anything further," said Milab.

"Oh, thank you," said the little girl.

"Absolin, I'll just pop Alisa down here. There is a big procession beginning soon from the Gates of Paradise, and I must be there. I'll catch up with you later."

Milab floated off into the distance.

9

A WALK IN THE GARDENS

ABSOLIN AND ALISA continued their walk in the gardens. They meandered along a winding path between multi-colored flowers of every hue. The colors seemed to become more intense as they came into focus. They strolled into a forest where a sweet perfume hung in the air. The trail wound around through green shrubbery as multicolored birds chirped and fluttered among the trees. They could see a lake in the distance. Light sparkled from its surface. Approaching them on the footpath, was a pair of Blue Principalities in long flowing robes.

"Well, Absolin, fancy meeting you…and what have we got here?"

"Hallo, Blue Principalities. Where have you two been? This is Alisa. Alisa, this is Amorath and Anslo. Actually, Alisa comes from a different time and place."

"Oh, Hallo Alisa, delighted to meet you. But what is a place, pray tell? I know a little about time already, but what is a place?" Amorath was the first one with questions.

"Well, it's a little difficult to explain."

"That's all right, Absolin; I can explain it from what I learned at school," said Alisa. "You see, the place where I come from is on a large ball shape which we call Earth. It is one of several large balls floating in what is called the Solar System. Because of the great distances between the balls, it takes quite a long time to get from one to another. At this time, my father has gone to one of the balls called Mars, and Absolin is helping me to get over my missing him."

"Now tell me, little one, what is a ball? I have no idea what that means," said Amorath.

Alisa looked around. She looked towards the trees beyond the sea of flowers. There was a grove of fruit trees with enormous round red fruit. The red fruit almost dragged the branches to the ground.

She turned to the group and said, "You see those big red fruit? They are what we call ball shape; they are round."

"Oh, I see," said Amorath, "well, it's interesting that you should point to those fruits. They are very special to us in Outer Paradise." He continued, "We call them The Extreme Energy Fruit. The Armored Seraphim eat these before their many eons of guard duty along the battlements. They never know when Demons will attack - or where. It was clever of you to notice them. They are an essential fruit here in Outer Paradise. So, what is Alisa going to be doing?"

"Well, we're just going to take it easy for a while and give her time to relax."

Looking down at Alisa, the Blue Principality said, "All right, the Alisa, I hope you two have a nice time. We're just headed for the Nectar Café for some Angel cake. We'll see you later."

1 0

THE EXTREME ENERGY FRUIT

ABSOLIN AND ALISA began to walk further into the gardens. There was a tall emerald forest on one side and a shimmering lake on the other. As they wandered further, they heard loud singing coming from the trees. Then, above the treetops, Alisa could see a line of shiny metal helmets bobbing up and down.

"What are those?" asked Alisa, "They must be very tall people."

"Those would be a troop of Armored Seraphim. They are probably singing because they are happy to be going to the Nectar Café. They'll be going for their meal of Extreme Energy Fruit. It's probably been eons since they ate anything. Because they only eat every few eons or so they are always very happy when the time comes. Would you like to go to see them?"

"Oh, yes, please."

When Absolin and Alisa reached the Nectar Café, the Armored Seraphim were already in a sunken area and taking their places at a long table on giant chairs. From where the Angel and the little girl sat, they had a good view of the long table.

The Armored Seraphim laughed and joked, their armor clanking and rattling as they moved. Out of nowhere, four muscular Powers appeared. They brought a huge red fruit on a tray and rolled the fruit onto the end of the table. At the table stood another Power who held a large silver knife.

Absolin pointed, "That is a red Extreme Energy Fruit."

Stacked beside the red fruit were golden platters. With the knife, the Power began to slice the fruit into thin slivers. He placed one on each platter. The platters were passed down the table until a platter with a sliver was in front of each Armored Seraphim.

"Is that all they're going to eat?" asked Alisa, "Is that all they get?"

"Because the fruit is an Extreme Energy Fruit, each sliver will give an Armored Seraphim enough energy to last for countless eons. They are the heavenly servants that protect Outer Paradise from Demon attacks."

"But it's so little."

Absolin insisted, "The energy in that fruit is so intense it's all they ever need."

Before eating, the Armored Seraphim sang a chorus. Then they picked up their slivers of Extreme Energy Fruit in unison and began to bite from one end. Each bite seemed to take a long time to chew and to swallow. Eventually, when they had finished the last morsel, they sang another chorus. Afterward, they all rose with much clanking and picked up their arms. Then they soared away over the treetops.

Absolin allowed Alisa to sit for a while thinking about what had happened and then said, "Let's have a nectar."

As they sat, sipping their nectars, Absolin could talk to Alisa in peace.

"I've just heard that The Cherished Son is coming to visit Outer Paradise. I'm sure you would be thrilled to see what happens."

"Who is The Cherished Son?"

"You will see when he comes."

When they left the Nectar Café, they began to walk along a shrub-lined pathway, past a sign that said: This Way to The Grand Hall of Relaxation. Soon they were following Angels of different sizes and colors and very muscular-looking Powers. These were all going in the same direction. It became quite a crush with so many bodies.

"We're nearly there," said Absolin.

THE PROCESSION

THERE WAS a great deal of activity happening outside the Gates of Paradise. A procession was assembling and the participants were taking their places. Getting ready were various occupants of Outer Paradise, as well as different heavenly servants from Paradise Proper. Lines were being formed that stretched from side to side across a Wide Golden Boulevard.

Armored Seraphim were the first to line up. They towered above the rows of those behind them. Those next rows were made up of Principalities carrying fluttering multi-colored banners. The banners represented the different entities and houses of Outer Paradise and Paradise Proper.

Falling in behind the rows of Principalities was the Outer Paradise Silver Orchestra. The musicians were medium-sized Angels, much like Absolin.

The rear of the procession was made up of rows of all

kinds of the occupants of Outer Paradise and Paradise Proper. It was a very varied group.

The gathering was hushed as it awaited the arrival of The Cherished Son. Then, at a signal, a platoon of trumpeters blew a fanfare.

An Armored Seraph called out, "Attention all, attention all, behold, there cometh The Cherished Son."

The Gates of Paradise flung open and the Outer Paradise Silver Orchestra broke into a rhythmic fanfare, "Blaa…chip, blaa…chip, blaa…chip."

Out through the gates stepped The Cherished Son, a towering figure who danced in circles to the rhythm. As The Cherished Son continued to dance, the rows of the procession divided in the center to make a path. He danced all the way to the front row, where he was flanked by the Armored Seraphim. These then joined with him in the dance.

At that point, the Principalities, and all those gathered at the rear began to dance and circle each other to the rhythm of the Outer Paradise Silver Orchestra: "Blaa…chip, blaa…chip, blaa…chip…"

Then the whole procession began to move forward along the Wide Golden Boulevard. The destination was The Grand Hall of Relaxation.

12

THE GRAND HALL OF RELAXATION

ABSOLIN AND ALISA had just reached the entrance to The Grand Hall of Relaxation when they heard the Outer Paradise Silver Orchestra. They looked along the Wide Golden Boulevard to see what was happening.

"Oh, I can see them now," shouted Alisa. "It looks like a procession marching towards us."

The metals of the Armored Seraphim flashed as they marched.

The rattle of their armor accompanied the "Blaa…chip, blaa…chip, blaa…chip…" of the Outer Paradise Silver Orchestra.

The Cherished Son held his place in front, as he whirled in the dance.

"That is The Cherished Son," said Absolin, "it is eons since I last saw him."

"Oh my!" exclaimed Alisa.

When the procession reached the entrance to The Grand

Hall of Relaxation, the rows broke up as it processed through the mighty doors. Absolin and Alisa fell in behind the last line as the procession passed by. The little girl picked up the rhythm and danced and laughed around Absolin as they moved along.

The dancing continued until The Cherished Son reached the front of the hall. Then, when he stopped dancing, all the dancing also stopped. He mounted a raised dais and sat on a high jewel-encrusted throne. The Principalities and the musicians found seating on either side of the central aisle, while the Armored Seraphim stood at attention on both sides of the dais that held the throne of The Cherished Son. Absolin and Alisa stood at the rear. The Angel lifted Alisa and tucked her under a wing so that she could see what was happening.

"All right then," boomed The Cherished Son. "Welcome everybody to our ceremony. I will get down to business right away."

There was complete silence as The Cherished Son boomed on,

"I have ordered three likely candidates, three Extreme Energy Fruits, to be brought here so that I may select the one that is to be processed into the Vacuum Dimension. The fruits should arrive at any moment."

No sooner had he finished speaking than there was a fanfare of trumpets at a side entrance, and four Powers marched through a side door carrying a bier on which lay a giant red Extreme Energy Fruit. The fruit looked exactly the same as the one Alisa had seen being eaten by the Armored Seraphim. This first bier was followed by another, and then another. All three carried a red Extreme Energy

Fruit. The three biers were set down in front of the throne where The Cherished Son was seated.

"Cherub of The Books, I need the Incantation Book."

The Cherub of The Books flew up from beside the dais holding a large book with a gold-bound cover. He handed this to The Cherished Son, who flipped through the pages. When he had stopped at a page, he looked at it intently.

Then, after a pause, he chanted an incantation in a high-pitched voice, "Inchin, binchin, glinshin, flinchin," his voice was quivering.

He pointed at a bier and said, "That one."

At that, two sets of Powers picked up their biers and quickly departed the hall through the same door through which they had entered. Now, just one Extreme Energy Fruit remained.

The Cherished Son boomed, "This Extreme Energy Fruit shall henceforth be named The Chosen Energy Fruit. Let this be done."

He waved his arms around and then pointed at the fruit, "The Chosen Energy Fruit shall become The New Universe."

Closing the Incantation Book, He handed it back to the Cherub of the Books. Then he boomed, "Dominion Cromonion, come up here. Stand in front of me."

The Dominion Cromonion trotted to the front.

"I hereby appoint you Master of the Ceremonies."

The Dominion Cromonion bowed deeply to The Cherished Son and then walked to the bier of The Chosen Energy Fruit. He stood beside it, and snapped to attention.

There was another fanfare of trumpets. The Armored Seraphim on one side of the dais broke ranks and formed two lines in the center aisle. They marched in place, as The Cherished Son descended to the aisle from the high jewel-encrusted throne. He proceeded to march in place behind the Armored Seraphim. These all then marched, left right, left right, out through the great doors of The Grand Hall of Relaxation. They left in the opposite direction from which they had come. The Cherished Son's favorites followed him at the rear. Outside the hall, the procession reformed and headed off along the Wide Golden Boulevard to the Gates of Paradise.

Remaining behind in The Grand Hall of Relaxation, was a detachment of Armored Seraphim, the Principalities, and the Outer Paradise Silver Orchestra. There were new duties to perform. Absolin placed Alisa back on her feet.

"Can I look at the instruments of the orchestra?"

"Of course," answered Absolin, "But be quick. There is a meeting in The Great Hall of Planning, and I may be on the committee. The meeting is due to start at any time. I will take you there when you're ready."

"Oh, I didn't know. Can we go there now? I don't want you to miss your meeting."

When they left The Grand Hall of Relaxation, Absolin stopped a floating Bubble. They both got in and were whooshed away towards The Great Hall of Planning.

THE PLAN OF ACTION

ABSOLIN AND ALISA stepped out of the Bubble and walked into The Great Hall of Planning. This hall was in the shape of an oval, and they descended into a sunken well. At the narrow end of the hall, there was a gallery to which Absolin and Alisa climbed. They took their place on velvet seats.

At the left side of the hall were Dominions of several colors, sitting in tiered ranks. On the right side sat rows of Archangels and average-sized Angels of different colors. At the far end of the hall directly opposite Absolin and Alisa was a throne-like chair on a raised platform. On both sides of this platform were seated rows of Principalities.

For a while, there was complete silence. Then, with a fanfare of trumpets, a now more stately-looking Dominion Cromonion, wearing a crimson robe and a crown-like head-dress, swept into the hall. The Dominion climbed to the throne-like chair and sat down.

"Welcome everyone to this important planning meeting."

There was a long pause while he shuffled some papers.

"At this meeting, we hope to lay out the whole process for the delivery of what is now called The Chosen Energy Fruit into the Vacuum Dimension. We will call the roll before we get started. Thank you all."

Absolin turned to Alisa and said, "Alisa, that Servant of Paradise in the crimson robe is the Dominion Cromonion. He looks quite different in crimson. I told him that you are a special guest in Outer Paradise. He will probably mention you."

After a pause, a Principality shouted, "All present."

The Dominion Cromonion then continued, "Firstly, I would like to introduce everyone to a special guest, a friend of Absolin. Apparently, it is a she, and the name is Alisa. According to Absolin, Alisa comes from a very different time and place. Alisa, you are most welcome to Outer Paradise."

"Welcome Alisa," the whole assembly shouted.

"Now, let's all be seated and compose ourselves before we begin."

Uriah the Archangel was the first to speak, "The last time a Chosen Energy Fruit was launched into the Vacuum Dimension; it was a disaster. As the one who did the planning of that effort, I take full responsibility for its failure. I failed to realize the destructiveness of Demons."

"Oh, don't blame yourself," said the Dominion Cromonion. "Although you were in charge, it was a team effort. It wasn't all on you."

Absolin stood up to speak, "I'm surprised anyone can remember so many eons ago. Anyway, I was also involved, and you are right; we did not realize the deviousness of the Demons."

The Dominion Cromonion leaned forward from his throne-like chair and said, "Look, we all know what happened. The last time we tried to launch a Chosen Energy Fruit, to begin a New Universe, we lost our focus. Everything went haywire; it was just a mess. We had to send out millions of Angels to clean up afterward. Uggh! I feel nauseous whenever I think about it."

"Hey everyone, I have an idea," it was a small Cherub wedged in next to an Archangel, "I think I've got it!"

"Come out here, little one, and tell us your idea. We need all the ideas we can get. What is your name?" asked the Dominion Cromonion.

The Cherub flew down into the sunken well and turned to face the Dominion, "Oh, Honorable Dominion, my name is Acibeel. I have a suggestion for the Honorable Dominion. I have reason to believe that at the previous launch, Demons were able to get inside the Chosen Energy Fruit to disrupt the atoms as they were being formed. I now think there is a solution."

"Let's hear it."

"Do you remember how Demons used to breach the walls between the Dimensions and cause chaos? Millions of us Cherubs were shrunk to microscopic size. We were able to get under the scales of the Demons to tickle them."

"Oh yes, I remember. The Demons were so tickled that they gave up their attack and retreated back to the Gates of Hell. I remember now."

"Well, Honorable Dominion, the same plan could be used now to ensure The Chosen Energy Fruit develops properly. We Cherubs could go inside after the launch to make sure that the atoms were helped to form correctly and were protected. The New Universe would begin properly," said the Cherub.

"Go on."

"Meanwhile, Armed Seraphim could drive off any Demon attack. Everything would work smoothly."

"All right then, I think you're on to something. We need to gather a billion Cherubs on The Great Plain of Recreation. They will need to be shrunken to microscopic size to become micro-cherubs. Oh, and you may thank me for coining the new name: micro-cherubs. Ahem! The micro-cherubs will be instructed as to what they must do. My old friend, the Dominion Onslom, can chant the necessary incantations to enable the shrinking of the Cherubs. I believe he still does incantations."

"So, let's do it!" ordered the Dominion Cromonion.

Absolin called out, "Do you think the Alisa can join the micro-cherubs? She says that she would really like to try a shrinking."

"All right, I think that would be acceptable. We will pair the Alisa with Acibeel so that the Alisa will be safe." He continued, "Now, Honorable Principalities here present, you must gather at least a billion Cherubs on The Great Plain of Recreation. Find the Dominion Onslom and his Incantation Book. The Cherubs must be shrunk to microscopic size. Everyone, please dismiss!"

The Principalities moved as one. They left the hall to gather the billion Cherubs to The Great Plain of Recreation and to search for Onslom and his Incantation Book.

Absolin and Alisa joined the exodus. They grabbed a Bubble to follow along.

14

THE SHRINKING

THE ANGEL and the little girl traveled down to The Great Plain of Recreation.

Alisa was talking, "I'm so excited, Absolin; my daddy sometimes took me to the lab where he worked. He talked about atoms and about how they were the building blocks of all things. They sound so mysterious to me. When I heard Mister Cromonion talking about shrinking the Cherubs so they could help the atoms, I was very excited. Hopefully, the shrinking will work for me. I will see the little atoms and make sure they are protected from the Demons."

"My, you think you will like that? You are a very brave, Alisa. But first, we have to connect with Acibeel. He will be your companion for the shrinking."

As they swooped over The Great Plain of Recreation, they could see countless rows of what they knew to be Cherubs dressed in white. The rows stretched away into the distance until they became just a blur.

"It looks like there are a billion Cherubs already waiting to be shrunk," said the Angel.

They stepped out of the Bubble next to the old Dominion Onslom. He was already standing in front of a podium accompanied by an Angel attendant.

When the Dominion Onslom saw Alisa he asked, "What have we got here? What is this?"

"This is an Alisa," replied Absolin, "We've promised the Alisa that she can join with Acibeel and the other Cherubs in the shrinking."

"Well, the Alisa had better hurry. Is that Acibeel at the front? He is waiting over there in the first line. I'm just about ready to chant the incantation."

Alisa trotted over to be beside Acibeel.

Just as she took her place, the Dominion Onslom found the correct lines on the page and chanted, "Ichbar…inbar…enchelendar!"

In an instant, where there had been lines of Cherubs stretching to the horizon, there was now what looked like a huge white sheet stretching into the distance. The Cherubs had completely disappeared.

Absolin stood stunned. In all his eons he had never seen anything quite like this. The white sheet began to gather into mounds and then rise up to form a large white cloud. The white cloud hovered above The Great Plain of Recreation, as though waiting for its next move.

Now that Absolin was alone, he decided to fly up from The Great Plain of Recreation to a Nectar Café high on the battlements. He was joined by his friend Anscar. They found a seat with a good view of the plain and a view of the white cloud hovering over it. Alisa was somewhere in the cloud. Absolin hoped that everything would go well for her.

45

15

THE PROCESSION ACROSS THE PLAIN

The Cherished Son's procession had left The Grand Hall of Relaxation. The dais and the jewel-encrusted seat on which The Cherished Son had been seated were moved to one side. A new procession was being formed.

The Powers who carried the bier with The Chosen Energy Fruit took their places at the four handles. They carried the bier to the center aisle and lined it up in front of the Master of the Ceremonies, the Dominion Cromonion. He had hurriedly returned from the Great Hall of Planning and was standing to attention just inside the rear doors of the hall.

A detachment of Armored Seraphim had remained behind when The Cherished Son's procession had departed. These now moved to take up guarding positions at either side of the bier. The Outer Paradise Silver Orchestra formed behind the Master of the Ceremonies and behind them was a troop of trumpeters ready to sound a fanfare.

Bringing up the rear were the Principalities carrying their banners.

The procession was ready to move. The trumpeters blew a fanfare. The Outer Paradise Silver Orchestra began to play. The procession marched out through the rear doors of The Grand Hall of Relaxation.

The hall was high on the battlements of Outer Paradise. To reach The Great Plain of Recreation, the procession marched down the wide ramp that zig-zagged to the bottom. When it reached the end, the procession moved out onto the broad expanse of The Great Plain of Recreation.

The banners of the Principalities fluttered in a slight breeze as the procession headed for the Invisible Barrier. When it got close to this, it halted. The Invisible Barrier stood between Outer Paradise and the Vacuum Dimension.

A fanfare of trumpets echoed across The Great Plain of Recreation. The four Powers carrying the bier with The Chosen Energy Fruit moved forward, flanked by Armored Seraphim.

When the bier had been positioned, two of the Armored Seraphim approached the Invisible Barrier. One drew his sword, and the other brought out a large disk. Four Armored Seraphim grabbed the four corners of the tapestry that stretched beneath The Chosen Energy Fruit. They raised the fruit into the air and waited for the signal.

The Dominion Cromonion, the Master of the Ceremonies, shouted from the rear, "Now!"

A hole was quickly cut in the barrier and The Chosen Energy Fruit was flung out into the Vacuum Dimension. The Armored Seraph holding the disk immediately placed it over the hole to seal it.

A sound like a muffled explosion was heard. The Chosen Energy Fruit could be seen expanding in the Vacuum Dimension. It expanded quickly, like a fast-inflating balloon. It was changing color at the same time.

The voice of the Dominion Cromonion, the Master of the Ceremonies, now echoed across The Great Plain of Recreation, "Hear this! Hear this! The Chosen Energy Fruit has been launched. We are beginning The New Universe!"

A great cheer went up, from the whole assembly which had gathered on the plain. Fanfares of trumpets followed and continued for a long time. All eyes were focused on the explosive expansion of The Chosen Energy Fruit, The New Universe.

16

CONTROLLING THE ENERGY

THE CHOSEN ENERGY Fruit was now unrecognizable as it kept expanding to become The New Universe. The white cloud that had formed over The Great Plain of Relaxation had arrived into the Vacuum Dimension from Outer Paradise. After hovering in readiness, the cloud swept down onto the growing orb and became completely absorbed through the outer skin.

When it got inside, the white cloud merged into a blizzard of swirling electrons, protons, and neutrons. The micro-cherubs had come to tame these particles and direct them into their correct orbits - as proper atoms. They knew exactly what to do. Each particle of energy was grabbed and correctly assembled.

The Dominion Cromonion, the Master of the Ceremonies had commanded, "There will be no mistakes."

Acibeel and Alisa found themselves in the middle of the organized chaos. They were surrounded by franticly working micro-cherubs. Alisa thought, 'Should I have done this? This is amazing, but I am a bit frightened now.'

She remembered seeing the Armored Seraphim eating slivers of Extreme Energy Fruit but could never have imagined that inside were myriads of tiny points of light. She kept her arms wrapped around Acibeel's waist and hung on.

When Acibeel noticed her tightening her grip, he asked, "Are you all right back there?"

"Yes, I think so," Alisa shouted.

"Just hold me tight. I don't want to lose you in this crowd."

When every particle, electron, proton, and neutron spun in its correct orbit, the micro-cherubs' work was done. It was time to leave the rapidly expanding universe and regroup into the white cloud. Acibeel and Alisa were swept along in the crush of bodies as the white cloud reformed out in the Vacuum Dimension.

17

ATTACK OF THE DEMONS

WHILE THE MICRO-CHERUBS were working to control the energy inside The New Universe, they were utterly oblivious to what was happening outside. Way out in the dark vacuum of space, the Gates of Hell had appeared. Swarms of Demons spewed out into the void. These had horns, stubby wings, and long tails. Their weapons were spears and tridents that emitted intense destructive rays. Armored Seraphim, who were normal size when they stood on The Great Plain of Recreation, grew into enormous warriors in the Vacuum Dimension. They formed a line between the expanding universe and the charging Demons.

With the swinging arcs of their swords, the Armored Seraphim slashed and sliced at the advancing line, cutting some Demons completely in half. The Demons following could see what was happening. They stopped, turned, and scurried back to the Gates of Hell.

The New Universe had been saved and continued to surge in size. As it swelled it knocked the Gates of Hell out of its way and out into the nothingness of space. The Armored Seraphim returned to Outer Paradise; their assignments had been successfully completed.

When the white cloud had fully reformed it followed the Armored Seraphim. It settled down on the Great Plain of Recreation and spread out like an enormous white sheet. The old Dominion Onslom was still waiting at his podium.

When the Dominion chanted the correct incantation, "Enchelendar…inbar…ichbar," the Cherubs instantly returned to normal size.

Absolin was already waiting for Alisa. When Acibeel and Alisa popped up to full size, Absolin welcomed his little friend with a hug. They thanked Acibeel for all his help. Then the duo grabbed a Bubble and rode to the Nectar Café on the battlements. Alisa had so much to tell Absolin.

18

THE VIEW FROM ON HIGH

DURING ALL OF THE HAPPENINGS, Absolin had been sitting in a Nectar Café, high on the battlements. He had been joined by Anscar a Senior Angel who sat beside him.

Absolin suggested, "Let's sit out on the balcony."

They then moved to another table for a better view. A Cherub brought them nectars while they waited for the drama to unfold. Anscar gazed out over the Great Plain of Recreation and through the Invisible Barrier.

"Look Absolin, there is a white cloud hovering out over the plain. Oh, and down below, a procession with fluttering banners. It's right beside the barrier."

They heard the faint sound of trumpet fanfares.

"Right," said Absolin, "They're launching The Chosen Energy Fruit. Look, it's expanding in the Vacuum Dimension to become The New Universe. I wonder what's next."

As they watched, the white cloud swooped out and down and vanished into the expanding globe. Later they saw something like a plume of smoke stream out of The

New Universe and reform as the white cloud. Absolin hoped that Alisa was safe and that Acibeel had protected her.

Once they saw the white cloud head back into Outer Paradise, Absolin knew it was time to meet Alisa. He excused himself from Anscar and flew down to The Great Plain of Recreation to greet his little friend.

19

CATCHING UP

WHEN ABSOLIN and Alisa had reunited at the Nectar Café, Alisa poured out her story about everything that had happened with the atoms.

"Oh, Absolin, it was so wonderful. First, I was with all these millions of Cherubs. They accepted me as if I was one of them. It was amazing. Then later, we were all hurled into the midst of a blizzard of whirling points of light. I guess they were the parts of atoms. They whirled and whirled."

"Did Acibeel look after you all right? I was worried that it would be too much for you."

"Yes, he did; I was able to hang on to him all the time."

"That sounds great." Then Absolin continued, "Now, Alisa, you've been so brave. You might like to take part in some other adventures. Do you think you would like that?"

"Oh yes, I'd love that."

"Do you remember Cromonion, the Dominion in the crimson robes? He was the Master of the Ceremonies in

The Great Hall of Planning, yes? He has just informed me that I must go to inspect the work of Cherubs that have been shrunk to become new clouds of micro-cherubs. These he is sending to several different eras to work on some special projects. If you would like to, you can come along."

"…As long as I'm with you."

"Of course, you would be, Alisa. Coincidentally, we would be traveling near the era in which you live. It should be possible to drop you off at your home. We shall see. What do you think?"

"Oh, that would be nice. When would we go?"

"They're giving me another Angel as a traveling companion. So, I'll have to link up with him first. Now, why don't you have some Angel Cake? You look like you are starving."

Just as Absolin was getting up from the table a small Green Angel was coming towards him.

"Honorable Angel, are you Angel Absolin?"

"Indeed I am. You must be my traveling companion."

"Yes, I've been detailed to accompany you during your inspections."

"Green Angel, this is Alisa. She will travel with us." Then turning to Alisa, Absolin said, "Actually Alisa, it is true, one of the eras we are going to is very close to the era where you live. When I have finished my inspections, we can drop you off in that time and place. I'm sure the other Alisas are missing you."

"I'm not sure I understand everything Absolin. But I'll do as you say."

"We will bring your own clothes with us. Before we

make the drop-off, you can change into them. You don't want to look too out of place."

"Certainly."

"All right then. We'll pick a Bubble and be on our way."

Absolin checked the Bubbles floating by and picked a suitably sized one. The three stepped in for the journey.

2 0

THE NEW ADVENTURE

Alisa, Absolin, and the Green Angel flew out in a Bubble over The Great Plain of Recreation. They flew to where Absolin knew there was an exit to the Vacuum Dimension. The Bubble was soon whizzing through complete darkness.

"I don't see any stars. Where are the stars?" asked Alisa.

"That gigantic globe we just passed, is where the stars are. They just haven't begun to pop out yet…they will."

In an instant, they traveled for countless light years in space but were traveling outside of time. Suddenly there were stars everywhere and they were passing a great glowing orange ball.

"That looks a bit like a Sun. It's so big and hot," said Alisa.

"Yes, that is a Sun."

"What's that in front of us now? Is there such a thing as a brown planet with blue spots?"

"Yes, there is, Alisa."

Before the little girl could speak again, they had swooped down onto the brown planet and stopped near a huge shimmering pond.

"Oh, there's a white cloud; I didn't expect it to be still here. Do you see it out there, Alisa, in the middle of the pond? It's right down on the water. The Dominion Cromonion's micro-cherubs are still at work."

"Yes, I can see the cloud, Absolin. Is that what my cloud looked like from the outside."

"Just like that, except bigger."

"What are they all doing?"

"Well, they're supposed to be getting life started here. Let's wait for a while to see what happens."

"Oh look, Absolin, the water is turning green just where the cloud is. What is that?"

"That will be part of what they are doing, the part we can see."

A green film was spreading slowly away from the white cloud, in every direction.

"That's it. They've managed to get life to begin. Now let's get out of here. There is more checking to be done."

The Bubble scooted away from the pond and rose into a bright blue sky. Suddenly the blue sky disappeared as they headed into a huge dark cloud. When they plunged into the cloud all Alisa could see was complete darkness everywhere. After traveling for a distance, the Bubble dipped below the cloud and dropped into a torrential rainstorm. Alisa could see water flowing down every side as it fell further downward and emerged into a clearing between trees. The rain stopped, and the Bubble hovered above the ground in front of a group of mysterious figures.

Alisa thought. 'These are like those little monkeys at Glasgow zoo'.

Near the Bubble, sitting on the ground, was a small white cloud. When the cloud lifted it revealed a small figure lying in long grass. As the cloud rose and disappeared from view Absolin began to talk to the small figure. He spoke in a strange language. The figure suddenly leaped up from the ground. At first it looked confused, but then it fixed its gaze on the Angel and began to answer. Its voice sounded as though a little girl was speaking.

Alisa was mystified and thought, 'What are they talking about?'

She felt like interrupting Absolin but decided not to. The Angel continued the conversation for a while and then, when he had stopped talking, the Bubble moved backward and was again being washed in the rain storm.

As it began to gather speed and soar up through the dark clouds, Absolin turned to the Green Angel and said, "Our Dominion Cromonion will be well pleased with what the micro-cherubs have achieved here."

They moved above the clouds and voyaged among the stars. Then Alisa spotted a Sun that she thought she may have seen before. When she looked down, the clouds had disappeared. Now there were no clouds, just blue – and green.

She thought, 'Where is that? It's in the shape of the Firth of Clyde.'

"Is that the Firth of Clyde?" she screamed, "I'm home!"

"Yes Alisa, it is the Firth of Clyde."

The Bubble zoomed down until it floated above the pathway in front of an apartment building.

"Oh, there's our street sign, Blenheim Court. Will I have to say goodbye now? I suppose this is the end of the journey."

"Yes, you are home, Alisa."

"I will miss you so, Absolin. I have to thank you for all your kindness. I will never forget you," Alisa stifled a sob.

"Oh Alisa, you're always welcome to be my guest. Give me a hug and dry your eyes. Some day we will meet again. Now go and have something to eat."

After a hug, the little girl paused and became quiet. She stepped gingerly out of the Bubble and turned to wave goodbye and blow a kiss. The Bubble slowly moved backward and then flew away above the buildings into the twilight sky. Alisa turned towards the apartment entrance doorway.

Her mother heard her come in, "Where have you been, Alisa? Have you been at the Coats Observatory all this time? Your supper got cold, so I put it in the Tabot. Now take off your coat and come and eat something. I'll warm your pancakes."

"Yummy, Mum! My mouth is watering! I'm starving."

THE LIONESSES

THE OLD CAPE Lion was attempting to roar, but what came out was a mixture of a growl and a whimper. The growl seemed to come from deep in the animal's throat. The terrible drought on the grassland veld was taking its toll. His age, and the fact that he had not eaten anything for three days, was beginning to sap his strength. The roar would have been intended to startle any game between him and the lionesses. But again today, there was no sign of game nearby, no antelopes, no gazelles, or wildebeest hogs.

The shadow of starvation hung over the whole pride. Unless there was food to be found, their survival was in doubt, with the youngest members dying first.

The lionesses of the pride were spurred to action by the growing hunger pangs that gnawed at their innards. They rose together and set off for the river. What had been a swiftly flowing current had become little more than a tiny stream. The lionesses began to pad along its bank. Perhaps an animal would come to drink. They passed a large carcass. A vulture was squatting there, still picking at the bones. Moving on they eventually spotted a lone gazelle down at the stream. The gazelle was drinking, oblivious to any danger.

Because there was no bush cover, the lionesses would have to surround the gazelle to prevent its escape. Suddenly the animal sprang up, startled. It knew there was danger. It began to bound away, but was too late. The fastest lioness was quickly on its heels. With one bound, she grabbed the gazelle's flank. The animal collapsed on the ground, where the big cat sank her teeth into its neck. The other lionesses were quickly onto the prey and began to strip every morsel of flesh from its bones. The younger members of the pride would not manage to get any of this food in the crush of bodies. They would have to wait for their big sisters to have full bellies before getting their portion.

The lionesses moved off again along the banks of the stream. They had explored along many bends without finding anything. Flocks of birds would collect in front of them but, at their approach, would fly away and disappear like a mirage. The big cats padded on, under the searing rays of the midday Sun. Then there began to be an unfamiliar scent in the air. The lionesses pushed on in the direction of the scent and, spurred by hunger, began to bound in that direction. They were running between two jungles when, over a hill, in the center of the dry grassland veld, was a pack of two-legged animals. The herd was almost stationary, as though waiting for the big cats. Driven by instinct, the lionesses slowed and spread out, to surround their prey. The pride might survive the season after all.

A TRAGIC END

TWO-LEGGED dark-haired creatures were emerging from the edge of a jungle. They struggled through a maze of branches and ground brush. Then, in bright sunlight, they grouped together and began to trek across a flat grassland veld. They were headed to the foot of another jungle, straight ahead. Before they could reach the cool of that jungle, one of these dark-hairs spotted a big cat stalking between him and the first trees. He looked right and looked left; big cats were all around. A pride of lionesses now surrounded the group. The big cats pounced and quickly crashed every one of the dark-haired ones to the ground. Each lioness found a neck to bite, beginning the death throes of their prey. Screeches and yelps filled the air. The group was doomed.

Just two adult males, and a young female, managed to pull themselves out from under a pile of writhing bodies. These ran in terror towards the safety of the trees, straight ahead. On reaching the trees, the adults thrashed their way through the brush and clawed their way up on branches. The young female could not keep up, so, on reaching the brush, she kept going. In fright, she ran straight into a group of mothers playing with their young. The female ran to the closest one and buried her head into the mother's neck. The mother dropped the infant she was holding and flung her arms around the shivering little dark hair. They remained like this while the other mothers walked out to see what had happened on the veld. There they froze in fright. When they returned, they grabbed all the infants and climbed into the trees. The little dark hair was helped up a tree and pushed onto a suspended deck of twigs and leaves. She lay there shivering in fright.

Later, sitting up, the dark hair began to speak in a tiny voice, "Crumm...Crumm..." but the mothers did not understand.

They looked at each other with questioning glances and grunted among themselves. They sniffed at the little dark hair's body and fiddled with her hair.

The males that had escaped the massacre had climbed to upper branches where they stared out through foliage to where the lionesses were still devouring the bodies of their fellows. There were no more screeches or cries. Apart from the occasional crack of a bone, a somber quiet hung over everything. Finally, when these survivors turned away from the scene of horror, they saw that they were being watched by other two-legs who looked at them through masses of leaves.

One of the survivors started to talk, "Crumm... Crumm..." but the words made no impression.

The other two-legs just turned their backs and swung

back into the jungle. The survivors shrugged their shoulders and busied themselves with sampling the leaves of this new jungle. Their companions out on the grassland veld were soon forgotten.

THE DARK HAIRS

THE TWO-LEGGED dark-haired creatures of this story were the Kee Persh. They would have been jungle dwellers many eons ago. The name Kee Persh distinguishes them from many similar pre-historic two-legged animals known to anthropologists. Anthropologists call a loosely-related grouping like theirs, a band. The Kee Persh were lithe and slim with strong arms and legs. Most of their body was covered with hair. The particular band in this story, that was almost wiped out by the lionesses, we will call the Dark Hair Kee Persh. They were heading to meet their long-lost cousins. These cousins were light-haired, probably because they had lived for many generations further from the equator. A typical Kee Persh face was not all that unlike that of a human, except that their features were not so sleek and rounded. They had flat noses and dark brown eyes in deep sockets.

The Kee Persh communicated with each other using basic sounds. Their languages were made up of grunts, growls and squeals. Although they mostly walked on two legs, their jungle habitat meant that much of their existence involved swinging from branch to branch, and moving from tree to tree. Adult males were about 1650 millimeters tall, and adult females were about 1520 millimeters.

For survival, the Kee Persh lived in the trees of jungles, high above the ground. This is where they were safe from the most dangerous predators. When confronted by an enemy, their only means of defense was to scream at it, or to flee from it. Occasionally, if one member was confronted with a serious threat, they would just move to another area of trees. But, in any case, where there was no jungle, there was no protection. The Kee Persh saw everything with tunnel vision. Much of their energy was focused on preserving each other, and the band.

This story is set in the jungles of the Southern African continent. The origins of our Kee Persh are necessarily shrouded in mystery, as is the length of time they had been living in their jungle refuges. Though the Dark Hairs and their light-haired Kee Persh cousins looked different, they shared the same genetic makeup.

The band, which was almost totally wiped out by the lionesses, was crossing a grassland veld to meet the other band of its kind. They may have been crossing to exchange mates or to find better food. This disaster, the fatal encounter with the lions, was unusual in that Kee Persh would not usually allow themselves to be exposed to danger in the open. Their group memory would remind them that they were always more vulnerable in open spaces, without trees.

JUNGLE LIFE

As soon as the first sunlight filtered through the leaves of their jungle home, the Kee Persh would look for their first food of the day. They would search for fresh edible leaves and any berries or nuts they could find. Mothers with infants would seek for tender leaves that they could prepare for little mouths. The members of a band spent all their time among the treetops. Over generations, they had learned that the safest place for them was among the topmost branches. The leaves and fruit of the trees gave them the food they needed. All their births, lives, and deaths took place here, and their lives were mostly peaceful.

Though there might be dangerous animals in the jungle that should be avoided, our particular Kee Persh were able to make friendships with other jungle dwellers. The mothers had built a friendship with the Sharp Tooth Lizards that lived along-side them. These provided a level of extra protection for the young. The lizards, by catching dangerous spiders and other insects, were able to add an extra level of protection. For their part, the mothers provided berries to the Sharp Tooths whose claws were no good for picking this fruit; their claws were mostly good for climbing. Whenever a Sharp Tooth passed a Kee Persh mother, it would have a berry popped between its jaws.

The arrival of the three Dark Hair survivors of the attack by the lionesses, was hardly noticed by the light-haired band. They had found a safe refuge in this new jungle and fell right into the daily routines. This was especially true of the little Dark Hair female. Though she did not yet understand the language of these Persh, she could see that there was a special relationship between the mothers and the Sharp Tooth Lizards. She would climb to where a tiny one was being fed, and watch as a berry was popped into the mouth of a passing lizard. The mothers taught their new daughter how to feed a berry into a lizard's mouth. In no time she had joined the mothers in caring for their young.

2 5

A STRANGE FRIENDSHIP

THE KEE PERSH band's strong friendship with the Sharp Tooth Lizards was formed after the Persh had fled to escape a plague of vicious Cape Monkeys. The band had been forced to move to a different part of the jungle for safety. The monkeys had often attacked the Persh, trying to snatch away young females. This was a real threat to the band, who needed to be very protective of their young. Now, in this new part of the jungle, they had been able to find safety and, luckily, to find the Sharp Tooth Lizards. The friendship with the lizards bloomed. The Kee Persh felt secure.

However, on one occasion, as it was getting towards sundown, some Persh, who were near a clearing in the jungle, heard a fearful sound. The sound sent shivers through their bones. The yelps that they heard could only have been made by the vicious Cape Monkeys. The monkeys had discovered where the Persh had escaped to and would soon be coming to try to capture young females. Sure enough, when some mothers and young females were bedding down in their nests, Cape Monkeys had smelled their presence.

A monkey burst through dense foliage at a nest and swung toward a young female. It caught the female by the arm and grabbed her around the waist. She screamed as it lifted her up and started back into the dense foliage. But a Sharp Tooth, clinging to a tree trunk, leaped sideways onto the Cape Monkey's shoulder and sank its teeth into the monkey's neck. Other Sharp Tooths appeared and grabbed the monkey's arms and legs. They sank their teeth deep into flesh. The monkey was yelping and flailing wildly. It dropped the young Persh female and turned to flee. As it did so, it ran head-on into other Cape Monkeys coming to join the hunt. These monkeys got the same treatment from the Sharp Tooths as teeth sank into unexpecting flesh. There was a great clamor of yelping as Sharp Tooths gripped the arms and legs of fleeing monkeys and the animals stumbled or fell to the ground.

Despite this victory of the Sharp Tooths there was the continuous fear that, at some point, the Cape Monkeys would get past the lizards and reach the young females. The Persh band was now living at the very edge of the furthest boundary of their jungle stand. There was nowhere else to go if ever the Cape Monkeys overwhelmed the lizards. The only permanent solution was for the band to reach the other jungle, the jungle they could see across a wide swath of grassland veld. However, their instincts told them of the dangers involved in being exposed on open ground. These instincts also told them that, during a crossing, only heavy rain would block the smell of their bodies from reaching the nostrils of roving flesh eaters. They would have to wait for the heavy rain of the rainy season to make their escape to permanent safety. The older Persh made the band bide its time until the first heavy downpour. They would wait and wait until the time was right.

The escape would be traumatic. This was the only jungle home this band had ever known. They had no memory of what had happened to their forebears. But it was time to move to a new jungle where there were no vicious Cape Monkeys.

26

A NEW JUNGLE

Dark clouds had begun to roll over the jungle dwelling-place of the Kee Persh band. The first downpours of the rainy season then began. It was time for the Persh to search for a new home in that jungle across the grassland veld. One sunup, the rains were a real deluge and would not be stopping.

An older male called out, "Graaak…grick…graaan…"

Every member of the band stopped what they were doing and, abandoning their leafy nests and decks, swung to the jungle floor below. The healthy helped the frail. Mothers popped their young under their arms as they swung to the ground. The band assembled in the undergrowth. They were ready to follow the older Persh as they moved out into the blinding deluge.

"Greeek…greeek!" the band struggled forward.

Soon water was cascading down every face and hairy body. All that the Persh could see was a wall of falling water, but they kept pushing forward. They had spent such a long time staring out at their longed-for refuge, that they could have found their way there with their eyes closed. They trudged on through the rain until, suddenly, where they had seen nothing but water, there was underbrush and the outline of trees straight ahead. After two older males had searched inside for danger and found none, the whole band thrashed its way through underbrush and bushes. They scaled onto branches and began the climb to their new home. Though dripping with water, the band was happy to be safe.

The first thing was to assemble nests for the mothers with young. Because of water dripping from the trees, these were built in any sheltered spots. The torrential rains would continue. The season had only just begun.

Slowly the Persh fell back into their routine of eating, sleeping and grooming. There was the kind of peace and tranquility among these trees that brought them calm. Though there would be no Sharp Tooth Lizards, their protection was not needed.

This peace and tranquility lasted until, soon after one sunup, there was the blood-curdling scream of a young male, "Graakee…"

The young Persh screamed in terror as a giant Cape Gorilla swung through the trees and grabbed him by the throat. The gorilla shook the Persh by the neck and hurled him to the ground. This first gorilla was followed by another. This one grabbed another young male by the throat before smashing his face with a fist and flinging him to the ground. These ferocious animals had been alerted to the presence of the Persh by their morning chatter of grunts.

The gorillas were likely expanding their territory, and these two-legged Persh were in their way.

Some of the band were still in their nests but the whole group heard the scream of horror. Their instinct for survival came suddenly to life, and they began to swing away, branch by branch, from the threat. They had to abandon their new home with all its new nests and perches.

Eventually, the band got far enough away so that the angry gorillas lost interest in the pursuit. When they reached the edge of the jungle there was nowhere else to go but down. They began swinging to the jungle floor. The males that had been attacked struggled out to join them. As soon as the whole band had gathered together, they moved out between the tree trunks. It was raining heavily as they set out to find another stand of jungle, and safety. They trusted that the rain would keep falling.

27

A STRANGE ENCOUNTER

THE FLEEING Kee Persh trudged through what was now a blinding rainstorm. The older males, who were at the forefront of the struggling group, could not see anything ahead. But the thought that the gorillas might be coming behind them spurred them on. They were still being deluged by the rainstorm when suddenly the sky above them became clear. The rain ceased, and the air became cooler. The Persh sensed a new danger and stopped where they were. Water was still running down through the hair on their bodies as a mist started to spread over them.

Some older adults grunted "Graaa...graaa..." in confusion.

The mist became a fog and then condensed into a white cloud. The cloud enveloped the Dark Hair female, the young survivor. She had been standing near the Persh mothers but she now became completely hidden in the cloud; she had disappeared.

Meanwhile, a huge translucent ball had emerged

through the sheets of torrential rain. It floated above the long grass and moved towards the white cloud. Inside the ball were three glowing figures hovering in mid-air. The Persh who saw what was happening stood in stunned silence or shuffled back and forth.

The white cloud lifted into the air and hung high above the scene. The young Dark Hair female was revealed, lying in the wet grass. She leaped up and immediately looked towards the translucent ball. There were three figures in a line, side by side. A tall figure stood in the center. It had golden hair, was covered completely in a long white gown, and had huge feather wings. On one side of this figure was another that was much smaller. It was like a copy of the large figure. It had wings, but it was green in color and was about the size of a young Persh male. The figure on the opposite side looked different. It had long dark hair and wore a shining silver tunic with a golden cord as a belt. This figure had no wings of its own but stood under a wing of the tall figure. Each of the figures had a face that was not all that unlike a Kee Persh face. There were eyes and a mouth, but the faces were smooth. All three faces radiated warmth, and the eyes glistened like stars. These eyes looked directly at the staring little Dark Hair.

"…Greetings Ahn. I bring you greetings from the past…and from the future. I call you Ahn because that is the name which I have been given for you," the tall figure was speaking. It continued, "I am here to tell you that you can now understand what I am saying. You can now speak the language that I am speaking. You now understand what is happening around you, and you can imagine what is happening somewhere else. You believe in the future."

"…Graaa…graaa…wha…who…who are you?" Ahn struggled to speak.

"Do not be afraid. I am Absolin, an Angel. I have come here to confirm that the white cloud has done its work properly. Its work was to change you into a being that had never become a being before. You are now that New Being," the Angel spoke with a sweet voice.

"W…w…will you take me away?" asked Ahn, wanting to know what was happening.

The angel replied, "You will stay with the Light Hair ones to help them survive. I understand that you will undertake a journey, but I do not know more about that. You have been given the gift of new light for your mind, and you have been given the gift of giving that light to others. Also, you have been given gifts for your body so that you will survive and endure."

"A…a…and…will you be staying with me?" asked Ahn.

"Our place is not here. Our place is elsewhere. We will depart now," it answered, and then, "Ahn, take good care of yourself…and the others."

At that, the hovering trio began to move backward in the translucent ball until it disappeared into sheets of torrential rain.

Ahn sat down on the wet grass. Her mind was spinning as she looked around to remember where she was.

"Where am I? Who am I with?" she asked herself, and felt as though she had awoken from a long dream, "Where did all these colors come from? Why is my hair so wet?"

The Persh were startled to hear her make these strange

sounds. They grunted among themselves. Ahn was using her new language.

It was as though she had always lived in a small box, and now the box had suddenly been opened to the light.

She thought, 'I feel completely different inside and so different now to those who are with me. I wonder what they are to me now. In my new language, I will call them the name given to me by the Angel. They are my Light Hair family.'

The torrential rain started to close in on the group. The older males led the group again through the deluge to find another jungle. As they pushed forward, Anh juggled a thousand thoughts and feelings in her head. She had to deal with a whole new world. Bright stars of every color swarmed through her mind in stark contrast to the gloomy downpour. Even the water flowing through her body hair had a new meaning. It was like a physical expression of something she had never known before. She was full of joy.

There was an assurance that the fleeing Light Hairs would soon reach the safety of another jungle. That all would be well.

The group struggled up a hillside and stumbled through longer grass. They struggled through brush and thick undergrowth before coming to the dark face of a new jungle. There was no foray to check for safety, just relief that shelter had been found. They trusted that it would be safe.

AFTER THE ANGEL

THE RAIN CONTINUED, as the Kee Persh entered their new jungle home. Their instincts were still shaken by the events that had happened to the Dark Hair female. They did not check for dangers; they just thrashed their way in and began to fill their bellies with leaves and berries. They ate like hungry lizards. The females popped morsels into the mouths of their young.

When the males had enough to eat, they built nests and other sleeping places. Since it was still raining, they did not build high in the treetops. They picked areas lower down that had less dripping water. They built in the way they had always built, and Ahn joined in the work. With her new understanding, she was able to help make better sleeping places. She could tie knots in twigs, something she would never have thought to do before.

"…You're doing a wonderful job, my little Dark Hair New Being. How happy I am to greet you…" a very melodious voice vibrated within Ahn. She stopped what she was doing…stunned.

This was another new experience for her.

She wracked her brain, 'Where is this voice coming from? Is this the voice of the bright being?'

The voice spoke again, "…I hope we can soon meet. I have so much to show you..."

Ahn was relieved; she spoke out loud, "Who are you, are you here? Where are you?"

But there was no reply. Though the words had vibrated within her, she felt they had come from somewhere very far away. She was glad of this voice though, someone, somewhere, was looking over her. She hoped that the voice would come back and say much more.

She named it "The Melodious Voice."

29

THE INSTRUCTION

THE KEE PERSH MALES had made a nest for the mysteriously transformed female. They instinctively knew that the Dark Hair one had completely changed, that she was something different. They sensed a new strength in her presence. When her nest was finished, Ahn, who felt utterly exhausted, climbed in, flopped down, and quickly fell asleep. She slept there, completely oblivious, all that day and into the next. Then, when she awoke, the first thing she noticed was the perfume of the jungle and happy birdsong.

She lay back, stroking the hair on her body. Then she sat upright to look at herself. Looking down at her front, she thought, 'I love how my breasts and belly are so smooth and warm and how the hair is so flat against my skin.' She couldn't see her face, but it also felt smooth and warm to her touch. She thought, 'Oh, how beautiful I am, and look, I am surrounded by so many colors, shades of green and brown. Oh, and trees stand around me in all directions where they disappear away into the dark.' She spotted that high above were patches of blue.

Her imagination was whirling about around her when it was interrupted by The Melodious Voice, "…My little New Being…" it said, "…you must join with the male standing above you on the split branch. You must mate with that Light Hair one only. I have given you the knowledge as to what you must do…"

Ahn looked up and saw a young Kee Persh male standing on a split branch above her. He was silhouetted against the early light, and she thought, 'He looks cute against the sky. His hair is so light-colored but I wonder whether I can do this. I'm still young and have only just reached my grown-up time. Am I ready? But The Melodious Voice says I must do it…so here I go! I feel that I have complete trust in The Melodious Voice. I'm thinking of the Light Hair word for help, "Grruu." so I'll call him Croh.'

She knew what she must do and swung up towards him. Ahn had noticed how the Persh were now very timid around her. She wondered how Croh would respond to her directions.

She grunted, "Graak…graak…" in Persh and pointed down to where she had been sleeping.

When Anh reached the bed of leaves, she lay down and made a hand sign for Croh to lay beside her. Croh responded and swung down to her nest. Her body shivered with emotion as the young male touched her for the first time. Tears collected on her cheeks when his eyes looked into hers. Croh became aroused, and in a short time the male and female bodies were locked in an intimate embrace.

Anh was happy and was certain that The Melodious Voice would be satisfied with their mating. As Ahn and Croh lay there, shafts of sunlight streamed from above. Bird song echoed through the jungle, and insects hummed everywhere. The pair began to nibble leaves and fruit. They were partners in a mysterious new relationship. Three of the Persh females crouched near the couple. They had watched everything. When Ahn noticed them, she was amused and smiled to herself. She named them, "Itsi, Bitsi and Kitsi". They were witnesses to the beginning of the relationship between Ahn and Croh.

THE WHITE FACE

ANH ALWAYS SHOWED LOOKOUTS where they were to keep watch during the day and at night. This helped her to feel safe. Sometimes at night, as she lay in her nest, she would let her mind remember the glowing white figure in the Bubble. One night, as she lay in her nest, she saw a white thing that would peek through the leafy canopy high above.

'What is that?' she thought, 'Why is it white?'

She rose up and swung her way to the treetops. When she found a branch to hang on to, she stared out through the leaves. There was that white thing out in the blackness among the many dots of light. Ahn saw that it was round and had a face.

She looked at the face for a long while and began to speak, "Oh, White Face, you seem so far away. Do you ever come nearer? Why don't you ever come to the jungle?"

Ahn was happy to be able to make new sounds and give them meaning. She was happy to have a new friend, but her words didn't seem to stir the face. There was no reply, only a silence broken by the faint cries of a distant animal.

Ahn kept watching as she said the name, "The White Face," and then, "what a wonderful sight you are. I feel so attracted to you."

She even sang a little song, but still, there was no reply.

She thought, 'I wonder if The White Face is where The Melodious Voice comes from.'

As Ahn watched, The White Face moved among the dots of light in the blackness. He began to dip down and finally dropped into distant treetops.

As he disappeared, she thought, 'Is that where The White Face rests? Is that where he has his nest?'

When The White Face had disappeared, Ahn swung down branch by branch to her nest and fell into a fitful sleep. On many nights, Ahn would swing to the tree tops to speak to The White Face. He would change his shape and sometimes not make an appearance but Ahn always talked to him.

"Oh, White Face," she would say, "how are you feeling? You look so different now."

There was never an answer, but Ahn would continue to talk. She would tell him about all the day's events with all the details. She would keep talking in this way until The White Face had dipped down into the distant treetops and gone to his rest. On one of these visits, Ahn thought, 'I must find the nest of The White Face…to find out where he goes to sleep. It will mean leaving this jungle and going to where The White Face lives. I cannot go alone. The Light Hairs will have to come with me. We will have to set off together.'

THE PINK FRUIT

ONE MORNING, when Ahn awoke, the sky was unusually bright. Light flickered through the uppermost branches. There was no dripping water. The rainy season was over. The Kee Persh had already built new nests and decks higher up in the treetops. But Ahn was restless. She sometimes wondered what had happened to the beings in the Bubble. She thought that she would never see them again. She knew it was time for her to set out to find the nest of The White Face. She imagined that this would be high in the topmost part of distant trees. She thought, 'The Light Hairs will have to come with me, but how will I get them to do this?'

One morning Anh heard The Melodious Voice within her, "…Go to the edge of the jungle. Look out to see what you can find…"

Anh went to the edge of the jungle with Croh. She stood looking out over the grassland veld. The line of tree trunks continued into the distance on one side and the veld stretched away to the foot of another jungle stand beyond. That jungle completely covered some low hills. Beyond those hills was a faraway white-topped mountain that reached into the sky. Ahn thought, 'That white-topped mountain must be in the same direction as the nest of The White Face.' She then noticed near her, just beyond the jungle, what looked like bushes of pink fruits. Ahn knew that the band would not eat anything that was not green, brown or red. But she thought that they might like these pink fruits as a treat.

"…Go eat, little one…" The Melodious Voice was insistent.

When Ahn had picked a fruit and used a stick to break off an outer shell, she discovered that inside was a succulent sweet fruit. She thought, 'I will use these as treats to entice the Light Hairs.' She picked a bunch of the fruits, broke them out of their shells and used a tray of tree bark to collect a number of them. There would not be enough for the whole group, so she would just try them on the males.

Ahn carried the pink fruits into the treetops, to a deck where there were some older males. She shared out some of the pink fruits and saw that they found them delicious. When Ahn swung to the ground again, she called out "Eh…eh…eh…" in Persh. All the males gathered around her, and she pointed to where the pink fruits grew. She waved an arm and they followed her out to the grassland veld.

Before introducing the band to the pink fruits Ahn knew that the males would have to find ways to protect themselves, and the whole band, when they left the safety of the jungle. They were vulnerable to all kinds of dangers, not the least of which being animals stronger than them-selves. Now was the time to train them to do as she commanded.

Ahn had the group sit down around her and began her lesson. She picked out one of the stronger-looking young males and motioned to him to come to the front. She had already picked a large pile of the pink fruit and had worked out how to open the hard shells with a stick. This pile was beside her as she began her next move. She raised her right arm over her head and motioned to the young male to copy her.

"Orgh…orgh…orgh…" she said but was met with a blank stare.

She raised her arm again and was met with no response. Ahn had tried the movement several times before the young male raised his arm. Anh stepped forward, patted him on the cheek, and popped a pink fruit into his mouth. The young Persh was still for a moment and then, as though transformed, let out a cry. He shot both arms into the air and danced around in a circle.

"Aaagh…aaagh…" he shouted happily.

Ahn performed the same exercise with each of the males until they had all learned to raise an arm in response to her. Each received a pink fruit as a reward. This obedi-ence training would come to be essential as the males learned to obey instruction. They would learn skills to help them defend their band as it zig-zagged across the grass-land veld on the way to the nest of The White Face. They would forget their longing for the leaves of their jungle. Instead, they would rely on Anh to show them which foods to eat on their journey.

Anh knew she had been successful. She had a new confidence and serenity about her plan. 'Wonderful, oh wonderful,' she thought. With her ability to de-shell the fruit, she could now get the Persh to leave their jungle home and follow her in her quest. The whole band would be with the males as they all joined her. They would know that they were going to a better place. They would follow their leader wherever she led them.

SELF DEFENSE

AT THE NEXT sunrise Ahn was joined by Croh, the adult males, and all of the Kee Persh band, right down to the littlest one. They gathered outside the edge of the jungle. Ahn arranged them in three lines for the trek. The adult males were assembled into two parallel lines. Between these lines was a line of the females and young. They would have some protection. The males were not armed, so it was very important that the column keep close to the edge of the jungle. In danger they could flee to the safety of the trees. They were beginning the first step of the journey to find the nest of The White Face.

As the Persh were used to eating much of the time, Ahn made sure that the group carried fresh leaves that they could nibble on the way. She herself carried a bark tray of pink fruits for a special purpose.

Just before they set off, Ahn took a final glance over the grassland veld. She noticed a translucent ball hovering in the distance. It hung there for a few moments before vanishing. Ahn would not be distracted and gave the order to go, "Graw...graw."

Moving off, the column trudged along on the grassland veld, skirting the jungle, loyal to the dream of their leader. They reached a downward slope and pushed their way through waist-high shrubs. Ahn spotted some mammoths in the distance though she didn't know what they were. They passed a herd of gazelles that was startled and ran away.

As they reached the foot of a hill, Anh saw that part of it had collapsed exposing an area of loose stones. She walked to the stones and bent down to pick up a sample. The stones were sharp and flat and would be good as a weapon for defense. Anh called the adult males around her and pointed at the stones. She picked up a stone, just larger than her fist. She motioned to the group to do the same. After several tries the males understood and began to pick up stones. Ahn went to each adult male with a stone to reward them with a pink fruit. Soon each one was carrying a sharp flat stone. They were now equipped for some self-protection.

"Now we must prepare ourselves..." She cut herself off when she realized that this was not in Persh. So she just said, "Grrh...gronk..."

The band started again in their lines, they were headed for the nest of The White Face. Ahn would find ways for the band to be able to protect itself.

3 3

WHERE TO AIM

Before the Sun reached its zenith they came to a new part of the jungle. This looked like a place where they could shelter.

"Grraan…stay here!" Anh raised her arms for the band to stop, before going into the jungle with two young males.

When everything was thought to be safe, the whole group entered. Anh noticed that, in one corner, there were young trees, just saplings, which were slender, straight, and tall. She knew that each male should have his own long stick to defend himself. Ahn clutched the closest shaft. 'These would be just right,' she thought, and paused for a moment to take stock. Then, clutching her stone tightly, she began to cut at the bottom of the sapling. One of the older males understood what she was doing and began to copy her on another young trunk.

The males were now sitting shoulder to shoulder among the trees. They were staring intently at Anh.

They grunted, "Grrh…grrh" in appreciation of what they saw.

Soon two slim saplings had been cut and lay on the ground.

Anh stood and looked at her handiwork.

She stretched out her arms in self-approval and exclaimed, "Aaaaah…this is nice."

She then hacked off branches at the top until she had a long straight pole. This pole was more than twice as long as a male was tall. A couple of the older males had already begun to hack at the branches, copying what Anh had done. Other males understood what was happening and began to look for their own trees. By nightfall several of the long slender poles had been formed.

Next morning the activity began again with more poles being made. Then came the training in how to use the poles for protection against dangerous animals. The males stood in a circle looking at each other with interest. Each one was armed with a cutting stone and a defense pole. They were ready for action.

Starting with the small animals that scampered around the jungle floor or scurried up and down the trunks of trees, Anh taught the males to use their new tools for defense. She was inspired to provide training both while being instructed by The Melodious Voice – and through her own wisdom and insights. The males were taught how to look for an animal's sensitive parts and to prod and jab until the animal became so uncomfortable that it would retreat and run for shelter. They learned how to hurt an attacking animal's eyes, nose, and ears. These are usually the sensitive parts and the parts most vulnerable to being prodded with the end of a stick. They also learned the importance of accuracy. It wasn't long before these skills would be vital in protecting the group. Anh looked at the males as they stood around her and before her. They were under her protection, and she was under their protection. She felt a calmness and a sense of achievement come over her.

The group took refuge there high in that jungle. Ahn chose lookouts to watch during the darkness. The next sunrise, after some time in her reverie, Ahn felt it was time to get moving again. She swung down to the jungle floor and called the Persh into action.

She approached the older males and pointed towards the way they would go, "Eh…eh…eh…"

She used the Persh sounds for "over there". When they understood, the band formed into its three-line column and set off.

THE GORGE

As the Kee Persh continued forward they came to a deep gorge. The column stopped in its tracks. Ahn, Croh and two young males stepped to the edge of the gorge and looked down. At the bottom was a stream that flowed between two steep, rocky cliffs. They would have to cross the gorge to get to the jungle on the other side. It was the only way. This meant climbing down one side of the gorge and climbing up the other. Ahn had two young males climb down to the stream.

When they reached it, they shouted up to Ahn, "Graah…graah…"

This meant that everything was safe.

While two lookouts stood watch, the Persh clambered down the first cliff face. The young and the frail were helped to descend.

When the whole group had crossed the stream, it was time to scale the opposite cliff face. Ahn first sent the two young males to the top to show how it could be scaled.

Then, the rest of the band began to climb. When some little ones that were being helped by females, were halfway up, there was an eruption of screeching above. A flock of ferocious hawks swept down into the gorge. With flapping wings and loud squawks, they swooped in, talons first, to grab for small bodies.

With one hand holding onto the rocky cliff and the other grasping a defense pole, the males already climbing on the cliff face prodded at the birds with their defense poles. The poles would strike a bird under a wing or on its beak. As a result, the hawks failed to grab any of their intended prey. Squawking loudly, one by one, they gave up the attack and flew away. The whole group was able to continue their climb and safely reach the top of the cliff.

A dense jungle was waiting for them. After a hurried check to make sure it was safe, the group disappeared into the gloom. Ahn decided that it was time for a rest from the journey. The males began to build nests to make their stay comfortable, for however long their rest would last. That first night Ahn climbed to the topmost boughs of a tree and looked out at the sky to find The White Face. Tonight, the face was fully round.

"Oh, White Face, how happy I am to talk to you again. It seems to be so long since I last spoke to you."

She poured out her heart to The White Face before climbing down to find a nest for a deep sleep.

A GORILLA ATTACK

WHEN AHN DECIDED that the band of Kee Persh were rested and refreshed, she announced, "Graa… graa…graa!"

The band swung down from their temporary home and assembled into the three-line column, out beyond the trees. Just as the Sun was beginning to climb into the sky, they left the deep gorge behind. Ahn had scanned all the way to the horizon to make sure that they would be safe. The column resumed its trek. The air was still as they began. The only sounds were the buzz of insects, the calls of distant birds, and the swish of feet through long grass.

Later, as the column passed an area of bushy scrub, there were loud shrieks coming from nearby trees. With a rustling of bushes and the crashing of branches a giant gorilla appeared. Ahn could not have anticipated this. The animal burst out of the jungle, waving its arms aggressively, heading straight for the column. Behind this first gorilla there emerged other fierce-looking animals, all shrieking wildly. The first line of males immediately lowered their defense poles and stood their ground. As the first gorilla reached the line, sharp poles plunged again and again into its eyes and nose. The animal spun around in pain and stopped in its tracks.

It whined loudly and rubbed its eyes, "Naaaa… naaa…!"

It swayed back and forth as it stumbled back towards the bushes. Other gorillas got the same treatment. They screamed and rubbed their faces and, after rolling in the grass, retreated back into the bush. The female Persh had moved behind the second line of males, but two gorillas had snuck past the prodding poles. These pounded around to the line of females.

The first attacked a female defending her young. It grabbed her defending arm in its jaws and threw her to the ground. Gorilla teeth continued to bite on her arms and legs. Older females confronted the other gorilla. It slashed at them across the face with its claws and across their throats and breasts. It then slashed at the young that they were defending. The male Persh had been taken by surprise, but then they rushed fiercely at the two gorillas. With their cutting stones they stabbed at the animals with all their strength. They aimed at arms and knees and poked poles into eyes and ears. The gorillas could not endure the attack. They howled and rubbed their eyes, and stumbled away, disappearing into the distance.

Now three adult females and some young males and females were lying wounded on the ground.

The young ones cried, "Yahh…yahh…"

Anh rushed over to the most badly wounded. The adult females that had been slashed by the gorilla's claws had blood pouring out of several wounds. Anh grabbed two armed males by the arms and ran towards the closest bush. She tore off a bunch of the biggest leaves and returned to place leaves over wounds, stopping the flow of blood. The remaining older females saw what Ahn was doing and ran to collect leaves for wounds just as she was doing. When every wound and cut had been treated with leaves, Anh realized that the wounded would have to be carried to safety. She chose some of the stronger males to carry them. Once the wounded were hoisted onto backs, and the very young were cradled in arms, they reformed the column lines as well as they could.

Some males stood at the ready with their weapons in case the gorillas resumed their attack. When it looked like the gorillas would not return Ahn gave a command to resume the forward trek. The group set off to escape the gorillas and to find a place of safe refuge.

The column progressed until the Sun was low in the sky. Ahn decided to check the nearby jungle for safety. She took Croh and two other males to scout. When there was no sign of gorillas or other dangers, the group pushed into the jungle and swung up into the trees. The wounded were carried or helped to climb. Ahn led the males as they built leafy nests for the wounded. These would need rest to heal and to recover. She wanted to get the wounded settled down before the light faded. Before complete darkness, every Persh had a place to sleep. Ahn took four young males, one by one, and led each to a perch so that there would be a lookout at each of four corners. She would be sure that the wounded were not disturbed.

THE FIRSTBORN

THE TREE TOPS where they had chosen to rest the wounded remained safe from the gorillas or other dangers. The wounded would be able to rest and slowly recover. While Ahn was helping them, she became aware that the swelling in her belly was a baby. She knew that she would soon be giving birth. When she had first mated with Croh, a group of Persh females had been looking intently at the pair. Ahn had named them as Itsi, Bitsi, and Kitsi. These three now sensed that it was time to get Ahn's nest ready. They gathered fresh leaves and some especially succulent berries for her to nibble. Ahn's labor was smooth and quick, and when Itsi had bitten through the baby's cord, they lifted the little one into its mother's arms.

Itsi, Bitsi, and Citsi sat around making approving sounds, welcoming the new member, "Gruu…gruu…" and "Graw…graw…"

Ahn began to suckle the newborn on her full hair-covered breast. The baby was a female and had the same hair coloring as her New Being mother. Ahn named her Ahah. Ahah was the first child of the union between Ahn, the Dark Hair New Being female, and Croh, the pure Kee Persh male.

The Melodious Voice spoke within her, "…Congratulations, my little one. How wonderful is the little New Being…how much like her mother…"

Ahn was delighted with her first baby; suckling the newborn took over her life for a while, giving her great contentment.

One day, soon after the birth, the three Persh females had been playing with Ahah. Just as Bitsi was placing the infant back into her mother's arms, a small bird flew past Bitsi's face. Bitsi was startled, and the infant dropped out of her grasp. Ahn had reached out for the infant and saw what had happened. She immediately scrambled down the nearest tree trunk.

Ahn was in complete shock when she saw that Ahah had landed on a rock and that blood was seeping out of a gash in the infant's head. She lifted the tiny one and laid her down gently on a mossy bank. Ahn's pain was everywhere in her body. She sank down to the jungle floor beside her baby, and lay there sobbing uncontrollably. Itsi, Bitsi, and Kitsi crouched close by, watching the mother and the little body.

The jungle continued as though nothing had changed. Insects continued to hum, and birds fluttered about tweeting their calls. Just one more life was seeping away in the jungle. As the light began to fade, a mist started to form in the trees above Ahn.

This mist became denser until it formed a white cloud

around the tiny body of Ahah. Itsi, Bitsi, and Kitsi had remained there, watching. They now stared in puzzlement at the cloud. Their eyes followed it as it rose and floated off among the tree trunks.

"Eeek, eeek…" there was an infant's cry.

Ahah's little arms and legs were waving back and forth.

Ahn popped up from where she lay, "Ahah, my little one. You are alive."

She lifted the infant gingerly into her arms and sat holding the tiny body, chuckling to herself.

As she climbed back to her nest, she sang a little song, "Little one, little one, welcome back to me…"

The mother and the child were together again.

The night air began to cool, and light rain fell on the jungle. One sunrise, there was a heavy downpour. The rainy season had begun in earnest. Water began to drip from the dome of leaves above. Ahn had the wounded moved to the most sheltered spots, though the feel of dripping water was probably soothing on healing limbs. Torrential rains came and went above the jungle canopy, and the air would become saturated with moisture. The Persh band sheltered as well as they could. The hair on their bodies meant that dripping water just flowed off, not wetting their skin. But they still preferred places where drops of water did not fall. If an adult got really wet, they would shake the water off their body, and drops would fly in all directions. A little Persh might find this amusing, but for adults, it was just part of living in the rainy season. During the wet season, the Persh would not venture out of their part of the jungle except to look for new trees with their favorite leaves, berries, or nuts. Otherwise, they were content to eat what was nearby, to groom each other, or to sleep.

The rain was very heavy one day as Ahn suckled Ahah.

She was interrupted by The Melodious Voice, "…It is time to mate with Croh… That moment has arrived…"

When Ahn was ready, she put her little Dark Hair into the care of the three Persh females and led Croh to her nest. When the mating had been completed, they lay together under dripping leaves. Ahn looked up at the slivers of grey sky peeping through the leaves high above, and she thought, 'I wonder what The White Face will think when he sees my little Dark Hair baby. He is sure to be happy.'

INTERRUPTED JOURNEY

THE RAINY SEASON WAS OVER, and the wounded had long ago healed. Ahn thought it was time to resume the journey to the nest of The White Face. One sunrise, she was awakened at first light and knew that this was the day. 'I'll have to make sure we are fully ready,' she thought. Reaching up and grabbing a branch, she tucked Ahah under her arm and swung down to a clearing among the trees.

She called out loudly for the whole band of Kee Persh to join her, "Graak…graak… Graak…graak…"

They all gathered with her in the clearing. A group of females collected nuts and fruits in bark trays so there would be enough food for the journey. The adult males held their defense poles and cutting stones. Everything was ready. They moved out to the grassland veld and assembled into the three-line column formation. As the column set off, Aaha was looked after by Itsi, Bitsi, and Kitsi. Ahn and Croh trekked near the front.

The column was moving close to the jungle when Itsi, Bitsi, and Kitsi moved up to be next to Ahn. They knew what was happening inside their Dark Hair leader. Ahn realized that she was about to give birth. She hadn't expected that she would give birth out in the open, on the grassland veld, with no cover. As they moved along, she looked ahead to see whether there might be a break in the dense undergrowth. The trees might not be so close together and there might be a clearing in the interior.

When she saw a break, she called out, "Grek...grek... stop."

She went with Croh and an older armed male as they pushed through the undergrowth and into the gloom beyond. They found a clearing between a mass of roots and branches and returned to the column.

Ahn signaled to a group of males; she pointed to the trees and called, "Grraa...grraa," meaning danger.

She waved the group through the undergrowth into the interior.

Then, when she knew they would be well inside, shouted, "Grek...grek," for them to stop.

On the grassland veld, Ahn spaced other males in a semi-circle, surrounding the females. Then just Bitsi and Kitsi joined her as she plunged back through the under-growth. The armed males were already waiting there as lookouts. The two females gathered leaves and reeds to make a bed.

When everything was ready, Ahn lay down and gave birth to a Dark Hair New Being male whom she would call Klint. After resting for a while, she got up, nursing Klint, and rejoined Croh out on the grassland veld. When the column had reformed, they set off, still in bright sunlight, to find the nest of The White Face.

3 8

A NEW SOUND

After the birth of Klint, as the column trekked along, they began to hear a booming sound. The booming got louder when they rounded a corner at the jungle edge. Ahn saw that they were approaching a huge rock. As they got closer, she saw that a waterfall swelled over the top. She thought, 'The booming is coming from that waterfall.' She could see billowing clouds of white spray hanging in the air.

The column slowed as it came closer to the rock, and Ahn gave the command to stop. 'There is no way forward' she thought to herself. 'We will take refuge here.'

When they had made sure the jungle was safe Ahn called out, "Graw…graw…go."

The column turned as one and melted through the undergrowth to the gloomy interior.

Later Ahn emerged with Croh and a group of young males. When they came out beyond the trees, Ahn scanned the grass veld and looked up at the rock. She wondered at its height.

"…Isn't it wonderful?" The Melodious Voice resonated in Ahn.

She was taken aback for a moment but then said aloud, "It certainly is most strange, oh Voice."

Then she thought, 'The Melodious Voice knows my feelings. It can see into my mind.'

She said out loud, "Oh Voice, you know exactly my feelings. I'm so happy to have you as a friend, but what is happening?"

The Voice resonated, "…It is because you are so special to me. There will be problems, but we will solve them and get to know each other completely…"

Ahn thought, 'But does The Voice know the obstacles I face? The sparkling waterfall and the billowing mists are pretty, but we must get around the rock. When will I be able to reach the nest of The White Face?' With such somber questions on her mind, she led the young males across the grass veld to scout for danger.

The whole area resounded with the booming of the waterfall. As the group got closer to it, the ground underfoot was wet. Ahn saw that as water crashed onto rocks, spouts of spray shot into the air. Cool droplets formed on their hairy bodies. It was a strange new feeling. As the group stood close to the waterfall, Ahn looked along the face of the rock. She realized that it continued as far as she could see.

She said the word "cliff" and saw that there was a wide track between this cliff and the jungle.

She thought, 'I wonder if large animals use that track as

they pass beside the jungle?' Ahn could see no large animals but she scanned the scene and wondered whether there could be a way over the cliff further away. But she could see no breaks.

Ahn then led the group to the bank of the river that flowed from the base of the waterfall. She could see fish below the waves, and in the sky above, flocks of birds.

Just then, a young male grunted, "Grraa…grraa…"

This meant danger, and Ahn swung around. Trotting along the path between the jungle and the cliff was a group of four-legged animals with long horns. They were headed straight for the group.

"Graak, graak" shouted Ahn and she led the group as they ran back to the jungle.

Ahn swung into the treetops and found a spot where she could look towards the river. They had run away from a herd of gazelle that had come to drink at the river. Ahn was relieved that those animals would never be dangerous. Already nests and a deck had been built. Ahn ensured that lookouts would be in place before she joined Itsi, Bitsi, and Kitsi. These three had been looking after Ahah and Klint. Ahn's heart had sunk at the sight of the towering cliff. But now she thought, 'I'll be looking after Klint and mating with Croh. This is a good time to stop and rest. When we find a way to get beyond the cliff we will continue with our journey.' Before the daylight had faded completely, the Kee Persh band and the three Dark Hair New Beings were secure in the treetops.

FIRST SEARCH FOR AN ESCAPE

LIFE near the waterfall continued and was uneventful. Then one sunrise Ahn saw that dark clouds were gathering and she sensed that the rains would soon arrive. She thought there would be enough time to search for a way over the cliff. Calling together all the Kee Persh males except those involved as lookouts, she summoned them out onto the grass veld and picked a group of the strongest and fittest looking. She got them to fetch their defense poles and cutting stones and assemble into two lines. She took up her place in the middle with Croh beside her. Ahn had already gathered a bark basket holding berries and nuts as emergency food. The group set off while it was still dawn and, at the waterfall, turned to follow the cliff face. They walked parallel to the dense undergrowth that grew at its base. The undergrowth would offer refuge if they were in danger of an attack.

When they had walked for a distance, Ahn noticed a gorge up ahead. This cut into the cliff face. On reaching the gorge, she saw that it began at the base of the cliff and sloped away upward into the distance. Ahn motioned to two of the fitter-looking young males to climb the gorge. When these had plunged through the undergrowth, they emerged beyond it. They climbed hand over hand up the rocky slope. Ahn saw they were dealing with stones that crumbled beneath them as they climbed. The gorge looked very unstable but the Persh kept climbing.

Ahn sent two more young males to join their fellows. Now four continued to climb. Now and then, a piece of rock would become dislodged and come tumbling down towards the undergrowth. In spite of this, they continued. Suddenly a colossal boulder began to move high above them. The boulder came tumbling down and hurtled toward the climbers. It skimmed past three of the highest climbers but caught the lowest one full in the face. He fell backward and lay motionless. The other climbers stood stunned and stopped their climb. They could hear faint cries of Ahn in the distance. She had shouted a warning, but it did not help. The trio retreated down the gorge to where their fellow climber lay. He was completely still, so they picked him up and carried him to the bottom. When the climbers emerged through the undergrowth, they laid the wounded one at the feet of Ahn. She knelt beside the body and looked for signs of life. Part of the skull had collapsed. There were no signs of life. The climber was dead.

The Kee Persh had a natural fellowship with one another, especially males of similar age. They did everything together in pairs or groups. This was for mutual support and protection. However, when one died, as soon as it was realized that life was gone, the memory of their fellow was forgotten. It was as though they had never existed; another male would take that place.

Ahn knew that the males would abandon the dead body right where it lay. However, she had a sense of respect for a member of the family of her ancestors. She instructed the young males to lift the body and carry it with them. Four of these gave their poles and stones to the others, then these carried the body back to the grass veld near the waterfall and laid it on the ground.

Ahn called all the Persh into a circle around the body, and when they had assembled, she stood beside it and crooned the Kee Persh words for distress, "Greeeeh… greeeeh…greeeeh…"

There was a long silence. Then the body was lifted and carried to the river bank. There it was taken to a sandy strip where it was lowered onto the water's surface. The swift current carried the body away. The group then returned to the jungle.

The experience of the death of the young Persh shook Ahn. This was a member of the family of her ancestors. Then she thought sadly, 'Finding a way to the nest of The White Face was not to be this time. But we will try again.' It was a long time before Ahn would attempt another search for a way over the cliff.

It was nearing the end of the rainy season when Itsi, Bitsi, and Kitsi helped Ahn with her second daughter. There were mild labor pains, but the birth was smooth. Ahn called her little one Alina. Alina was a Dark Hair New Being like her mother.

The Melodious Voice spoke within her, "…Congratulations on the arrival of the little one. The little Dark Hair New Being looks very like her mother..!"

As she suckled Alina, she replied out loud, "Oh thank you oh Voice, I hope she makes you happy."

The Melodious Voice continued, "…I will await you, no matter how long it takes…"

Ahn then thought, 'I hope The White Face will also be happy when he sees Alina.' As she settled into the habit of suckling the newborn, Ahn dreamt of the day that they could leave the cliff and the waterfall behind.

WALKING LESSONS

Her young offspring were taking over more of Ahn's life. The mother spent time nursing Alina, the newest little one, and teaching Aaha and Klint to speak her language. Aaha could already pronounce many words, and Klint had passed beyond the 'Mama' and 'Dada' stages. But there was always learning to be done. Croh could not help with the teaching, but he would wait patiently nearby during every lesson.

Ahn had already mated with Croh again and was expecting her fourth Dark Hair New Being child.

One day after a teaching time, The Melodious Voice spoke within Ahn, "…the little New Beings must learn to stand upright so that all New Beings to come will stand upright…"

After a pause, she thought, 'Very well, oh Voice. I will do that.' Anh really wanted a long rest but realized that she now had a new task. A fresh idea came to her as she thought about the problem, 'Why not build an enclosed area where it was safe to be on the ground? Aaha and Klint could learn to stand upright when they walked.' Klint was already able to walk on thick branches, but Ahn knew that he and Aaha would need the flat ground to learn to walk properly, standing completely upright. She came up with a plan. She remembered the tall, straight saplings the male Persh used as defense weapons. If she could find some stands of these, she could build a protective wall on the ground for Aaha and Klint. She swung down to the ground and called the males from their perches.

"Graak…graak…" she called, and the males came and gathered around her.

All eyes were on their leader. Ahn grabbed two defense poles and held them side by side as she struck them onto the ground. She then made a broad sweeping gesture pointing to the surrounding jungle. An older male came forward and took a pole from Ahn's hand. He thumped it into the ground, thump, thump, thump, at close spaces to indicate many poles put side by side. She thought, 'Great, you understand what I want.'

Then she said, "Graw…graw…" meaning go, to encourage the group.

The males disappeared into the jungle in all directions. Ahn hoped that there would be enough long saplings, cut to the same size and that the males would bring them back to her.

By the following sundown there was a pile of poles, mostly about the same length, at the base of a tree. They were piled high beneath the leafy deck where Ahn had been sleeping. At sunrise, Ahn was already cutting a trench with a cutting stone. It was in the shape that she wanted for a stockade. This stockade would surround a tree that was right at the edge of the jungle. On one side of this tree, there would be a space wide enough for Aaha and Klint to be taught to walk upright.

Ahn called the available Persh together to show them what she wanted them to do. First, she taught them to tie knots. This was difficult; only a couple of the older males and some females could master the trick. Apart from picking their food from trees or for grooming, the Persh did not use their fingers for tiny movements. Taking two poles, Ahn tied them together, top and bottom, with lengths of vine that she had gathered. She then added other poles, one after the other, side by side, connecting them all in the same way. Soon there was a row of poles tied together, which stood in the trench. With the help of the older males and females, Ahn was able to complete a safe enclosure, just as she had hoped.

Because the stockade had a continuous wall, there was only one way to get inside. That way meant climbing down the tree in the center. Now, with the help of Itsi, Bitsi, and Kitsi, Ahn would carry Alina down to the ground. Aaha and Klint would climb down by themselves, to begin their standing straight lessons and learning Ahn's language. Alina would begin to walk, and in between lessons, she would be nursed. Croh kept watch outside the stockade. He would warn if there was danger. Ahn's plan was a great success.

Every sunrise, Itsi, Bitsi, and Kitsi would wake Ahn early. They would help her carry Alina down to the ground for lessons and to play. Ahah and Klint would make their own way.

Ahah loved to chatter with her mother and ask clever young female questions, "How is it that we can speak, but the Light Hairs only say simple words? Daddy hardly says anything…is he a Light Hair?"

"Well, Ahah yes, your father is a Light Hair. He is the Light Hair I chose to be the father of all you little Dark Hairs, you and Klint and Alina. The Light Hairs never had the gift of talking as you and I have. We are different in a lot of ways."

"Will you be able to teach Daddy how to speak our language? I would love to hear him."

"No, I would not be able to. Do you notice how Daddy needs me to decide for him many things that he does? He is only able to make simple decisions by himself. You see, that is what the Light Hairs do; they only make the decisions that help them to survive," her mother answered.

"But I love the way Daddy is always by your side Mum; it makes me feel so safe. I can see that you do his thinking for him. I guess that's all right."

"Now, Ahah, it is time for our talking and walking lessons. Can you move over beside your brother while I see how little Alina is doing?"

EXPLORING THE RIVER

AHN HAD NOTICED that some of the younger Kee Persh males would look longingly towards the river and seemed to want to explore it. Early one daylight, she fed her little ones and made sure that Alina was safe in the care of Itsi, Bitsi, and Kitsi. She then gathered the more restless young males and had them get their defense poles and cutting stones. They all set off for the river accompanied by Croh. They reached the banks of the river some distance from the waterfall. Ahn knew that the river was fast flowing but also that there was a sandy strip where it was safe to step down and walk beside the flow.

When they arrived at the sandy strip, Ahn picked two of the males to be on watch. The rest of the group continued on. As they walked some of the males dipped their hands into the water and found it to be cool.

There was an approving Persh sound, "Shaaa…!"

The group walked further along to a pool which lay off the main current. This flowed more slowly than the river.

As they approached the pool, they heard the sound of whimpering and whining just ahead. They came across a four-legged animal lying on its side. Blood oozed from a wound onto the sand. Flies buzzed around the wound and around the animal's eyes. The animal looked as though it had tried to reach the river's edge but had collapsed before reaching the water. Now its tongue hung out, and it lay there, panting weakly. Ahn saw an eye looking pleadingly up at her. She did not know that this was a male Red Wolf and that it would have been very dangerous if it had been able to move. Our trusting Dark Hair female was unaware of the danger. Ahn knelt down at the water's edge to scoop water into her cupped hand. Leaning over she sprinkled water onto the animal's tongue. When Ahn had done this a couple of times, she realized that the hollow gourd that she kept in her nest would be very helpful.

"Let's go back to the refuge and get my gourd," she said out loud and then, "Graak..graak." meaning "come" in Persh.

The group followed her as they trooped back to where Ahn's nest hung high in the trees. With the gourd, they returned to the river. Ahn was now able to pour plenty of water into the animal's mouth, over its wound, and over its head and body. After this, the group departed and left behind a very wet animal. They returned to the jungle to eat leaves, berries, and nuts and to do some mutual grooming.

The next sunrise Ahn wanted to see whether the wounded animal at the river needed more water. Accompanied by Croh and a group of armed males, she set off for the river bank. She brought her gourd. When they reached the place where the animal had been, there was nothing but a large stain of dried blood in the sand. The animal had gone. Ahn thought, 'It must have recovered and returned to its nest. I wonder what could have wounded the animal. I hope we never meet that monster.' While the Sun was still climbing into the sky, they returned to the jungle.

A CLOSE ENCOUNTER

ANOTHER DAY, Ahn was sitting out on the grass veld, playing with Alina. She was joined by the Persh mothers and their young. Sunlight was shining directly onto the upper part of the great falls. Dancing colors sparkled on the cascading water. Ahn marveled at the sight. Nobody noticed when a fearsome-looking pack of Red Wolves rounded the edge of the jungle and trotted to the grassy area in front of the group.

The wolves stopped, then sank down onto the grass. The two largest had dropped down first, and then a group of other wolves behind them. Ahn and the Persh mothers froze in terror. They all clutched their young ones closely to protect them. They sat very still, waiting for the wolves to attack. The air was deathly quiet as the largest wolf rose and walked slowly to where Ahn sat with Alina. The wolf lay down in front of Ahn and bowed its head to the ground. Ahn realized that this was the animal they had helped by the river.

To calm the animal and herself she said softly, "Grihh… grihh……grihh..."

The wolf blinked and then rose onto its paws. It came slowly forward and nuzzled its nose against Ahn's leg. Ahn froze again and pulled Alina more tightly to her side. After nuzzling its nose against Ahn, the wolf rose and turned around. It headed slowly back to the pack. When the wolf reached the pack, it dropped to its previous position, its head pointed toward Ahn. Eventually, the whole pack of wolves rose as one and headed back the way it had come.

As Ahn and the Persh mothers watched, the wolves trotted into the distance and disappeared around the corner of the jungle. Straight away the mothers grabbed their young and vanished into the jungle undergrowth. They were terrified. Ahn was stunned. She had no idea why the animals had behaved in such a frightening way. She thought, 'What were those animals doing? Do they no longer see us as their food?'

During the remainder of that dry season and throughout the rainy and dry seasons to come, Ahn came to understand what had so changed. Whenever a large animal, such as a lioness, came anywhere near to herself or to her Dark Hair offspring or to any of the Persh, the wolves would appear out of nowhere. They would stand ready before the threat, glaring at it. If the threatening animal did not retreat, the whole pack of wolves would growl and bark menacingly. The threatening one would turn tail and slouch away toward its den.

43

SAVED BY THE RED WOLVES

ONE DAY AHN noticed that less and less water was flowing over the cliff at the waterfall. Eventually, at the end of a dry season, the waterfall had become a trickle. She saw that the river was now possible to cross. Low islands of sand were dotted from one bank to the other. It was time to search in a new direction to find a way over the cliff. At the next first gleams of light, she called the Kee Persh band out onto the grass veld in preparation for an expedition.

"Graak...graak...graak," she called.

The males, and some of the females, filtered down from the treetops. When the group had gathered, Ahn arranged an expedition party in the old column formation. Armed males were gathered into two lines; females moved between the lines for protection.

"Ahah and Klint, you will come with me. Be sure not to lose your grass skirts when we march."

From a young age, Ahah and Klint had always worn a

grass skirt. This was at the insistence of Ahn, who had never forgotten the command of The Melodious Voice.

The Voice had said, "…The Dark Hair New Beings must never mate with any Light Hair being. They must only ever mate with other New Beings. There must always be that separation…"

Ahn had invented the grass skirt as a sign that the command of The Melodious Voice would always be in force. As they grew, Ahah and Klint had learned never to be without their grass skirt symbol of separation.

When Ahn saw that the old column formation had been remembered and that the Persh were getting in line, she explained to her offspring what was about to happen, "Ahah, Klint, we hope to find a way over the cliff this time. I want you two to stay close together and to stay near me. Croh will be with us. Klint, you will carry a defense pole and a cutting stone. You must be armed for the search like any Light Hair male."

"Why do we need to find a way over the cliff? What is wrong with staying here?" asked Aaha.

"My darling, we have to find a way over the cliff. I must find the nest of The White Face," Ahn continued, "It pains me that my journey has been interrupted for all these many seasons. Does that answer your question?"

"Yes, Mama dear."

"All right then. Let us be on our way."

They set off across the river in the triple line formation. The water was shallow and easy to cross. Then, striding through long grass, they passed beside the dense bush that grew at the foot of the cliff. The cliff stretched into the distance. The Sun was still climbing to its zenith when suddenly a group of wildebeest hogs ran out of bushy undergrowth nearby. Flailing tusks flashed towards the first line of Persh. The males tried to aim their defense poles. The wildebeest hogs had almost reached them when, out of nowhere, Red Wolves came howling and growling. They leaped onto the backs of the leading hogs. Horrible squeals and snorts rang out as fangs sank into flesh. The squealing and honking continued until the hogs turned tail and scampered back to the bushy undergrowth.

Ahn was so thankful for the wolves. It might have been a catastrophe had they not arrived. They may have saved the lives of her son and daughter. They were safe.

A TERRIBLE ROCK FALL

THE COLUMN RESUMED the marching lines and continued the trek. Ahn scanned the cliff ahead. She hoped to find a way over before the Sun reached its peak. Then, just ahead, she saw a chasm that cut into the face.

Ahn called out in Persh, "Grek…grek…stop."

The group stopped and turned, and pushed into the dense bush. Struggling through, they emerged at the foot of an opening in the cliff face. The floor of the chasm rose in a long slow slope until, in the distance, Ahn could see that it reached the very top. The group began to climb up the slope between towering cliffs on each side. The only sounds were the echoes of bird cries back and forth and the buzz of insects in the dry air. Suddenly there was a loud cracking sound high above.

In a moment, slabs of cliff face had become detached and came crashing down toward the group. Rock after rock tumbled down in clouds of dust. The males on the side of the rockfall never saw the danger coming. There was no time to escape. They disappeared under the mass of rocks.

The remaining Persh cried out in fright, "Grraa… grraa…

They scattered out of the way through the dust. Ahn and her children coughed, spluttered, and stumbled away to where the survivors gathered.

They heard cries of "Greeeh…greeeh…" and moaning coming from the bottom of the pile.

When the dust had cleared a little, Ahn could see a body lying on the ground as if trapped. 'That must be Croh?'

She turned to her children, "Wait here while I see what is happening."

Stumbling back through the dust, she came upon a male lying on his side with his legs caught beneath the rubble. But it wasn't Croh. Where was Croh? Ahn's heart sank.

"Where is my Croh? Where is the father of my children?" she shrieked as tears welled up in her eyes.

She was devastated, but then her female instincts were able to take over. Through her tears, she looked down at the trapped Persh.

She called to Klint and the other males, "Graak, graak…quick, quick, help me get the rocks off his legs."

Together they were able to move the stones, but the wounded one's legs looked horribly crushed. He would have to be carried. There was no sign of Ahn's beloved Croh. Where he should be were just piles of huge grey rocks.

A feeling of terrible loss came over the Dark Hair mother. She began to cry in great sobs and reached for

Klint. Ahn held her son in her arms and buried her head in his shoulder. Aaha came, and threw her arms around her mother and brother, and joined in their sobbing. The surviving Persh, covered in dust, stood looking at the fallen boulders, unable to understand. They knew something terrible had happened but would never know that their brothers and cousins were gone forever.

They whined in sympathy with the sobs of the Dark Hairs, "Greeeh…greeeh…"

The survivors remained like this for some time. Then, when Ahn became more composed, she got four Persh males to carry their wounded brother by his arms and legs.

The sad group stumbled out from the chasm and pushed their way through the bush to the grass veld beyond. Red Wolves were still roaming around. The column would be protected from the wildebeest hogs. The Persh formed their lines as well as possible, and the group headed back to their jungle home. The wounded survivor would be lifted to a leafy deck to recover from his wounds.

4 5

———

A SADNESS AND JOY

IT WAS in very broken column ranks that Ahn, Ahah, Klint, and the surviving Kee Persh trudged back to the river. They walked through the shallow water near the waterfall and looked to see that the grass veld was safe. They returned to their jungle refuge without Croh or the other missing males. Some adult females came to meet those arriving. They were bewildered when they could not see all the males. They would never know of the calamity that had taken place. When she reached her home high in the treetops, Ahn threw herself onto a leaf deck. She grieved for Croh, the father of her children, and felt the pain of the bond between them now broken. A feeling of loss would stay for a long time.

Later, Ahn gathered Klint, Aaha, Alina, and Kraat, her second son, and told the two younger ones, "Your dad is dead. A pile of huge stones fell on him and some of his brothers. He was completely buried. We had no way of finding him."

Ahah and Alina flung their arms around their mother's neck.

"Oh, Mama," Alina cried, "we are so sad for you."

Ahn shared some tears with her little ones until she became more composed.

She said, "We will continue our time here, always aware that we will not be so safe. There are fewer Light Hair defense poles to guard us. You two Dark Hair males will have to carry poles from now on."

"Can we go to see where our father is buried?" asked Alina, "I would so much like to see the place."

"It is much too dangerous," replied Ahn, "If it hadn't been for the wolves protecting us, we might have been killed by hogs."

Just as she had finished, The Melodious Voice spoke within her, "...the young male and female New Beings must mate together. It is time..."

'This is a shock,' thought Ahn, 'I have just lost Croh, and now this...'

The Melodious Voice spoke again, "...This must happen now..."

Ahn felt the urgency of The Melodious Voice, so she said, "Alina and Kraat please go to your nests. I must speak to Ahah and Klint alone."

When the two had left, Ahn began, "Ahah and Klint, you know there is never to be mating between Dark Hairs and the Light Hairs. You know that you two were never permitted to mate until I commanded it. That time has now arrived, and Dark Hair must mate with Dark Hair. I now command you two, Ahah and Klint, to mate with each other. This must take place as soon as possible. You must join with each other in a nest near the decks of the females. When you lie down together, it must be as though you are grooming each other, Klint's body will respond to you Ahah, and you two must continue until you have mated. Afterward, you will continue to wear your grass skirts."

"Yes, Mother," said Ahah.

The two headed for the nest as Ahn had instructed. Ahah and Klint already shared a close friendship as they had been born only one season apart. They both had distinctive dark body hair, which gave them a shared identity. Before the next sunup, their mating was complete and a new kind of relationship had begun.

There had long been a morning ritual by Ahn and her Dark Hair children and many of the Persh. They would head off into the jungle to find breakfast and collect food for the day. They would have the protection of many male Persh with defense poles and cutting stones. Now there were fewer armed male Persh. Klint and Kraat now carried defense poles and cutting stones. Ahn taught them the uses of these for defense, just as she had the male Persh, so many seasons ago.

UP AMONG THE STARS

Hᴏᴛ, dry seasons followed rainy seasons in a slow rhythm. It might be thought that Ahn's life would be monotonous and lonely, but everything still looked so new to her that she was always in awe. She loved the Kee Persh, the sons and daughters of her ancestors, and of course, she dearly loved her little Dark Hairs. She was constantly happily surprised in her life and loved the times that she could talk to her friend, The White Face.

Many nights, when darkness fell, Ahn would climb to the upmost branches and look out through the leaves at the sky. She would look for the shining of The White Face. When she found him, she would practice her language. She knew he could always hear her and understand what she was saying. He would listen lovingly as she poured out her heart in her own words. She would sway back and forth on a branch, rocking in the arms of The White Face, even on the occasions when he appeared only partially. But the times she loved the best were when The White Face seemed to be right in front of her, as though she could reach out and touch him.

She would say, "Oh, thank you, White Face, for being there and hearing me. You know exactly my thoughts and feelings. I cannot wait to find the nest where you live." When she got tired, she would say, "Goodbye, oh White Face."

Then Ahn would swing down to her nest and fall fast asleep. Part of her hoped that The Melodious Voice within her was the voice of The White Face, though she never heard The Melodious Voice when talking to The White Face. The Voice only spoke at the times of its mysterious choosing.

4 7

AN INTERRUPTED LESSON

WHEN AHEE, Ahn's third granddaughter, had begun to talk and Ahn's third grandson Keel, had begun to walk, it was time for Ahn to resume her lessons. She could swing down from her leafy deck to where Ahee and Keel were being attended to by their mothers, Alina and Ansoa. Bitsi and Kitsi, were there. Itsi had passed away.

"Well, happy sunrise, everyone! How are we all?" Ahn scooped up Ahee in her arms and rocked her back and forth.

"Nanaa…nanaa," already the little one had begun to speak Ahn's language.

They sat around in the stockade where they were joined by Aloa, Ahn's first granddaughter.

Ahn asked, "How did you sleep, Aloa?"

"I was a little restless. I think the new little one will arrive soon. I feel a lot of movement, and I can tell that Bitsi and Kitsi are aware and will help," replied Aloa.

"Well, let's wait and see," said Ahn. "Go to your nest

136

and rest as much as possible. Your baby will be my first great-grandchild and I am so excited! I will make sure that Klint will gather you some extra food."

Ahn doted on her grandchildren but with a great-grandchild, her love would be extra special. She uncurled Ahee's arms from her neck and sat her down on the ground next to her.

"Now it is time for a lesson in my language. Let us begin…"

So began that day, which was to be the first of many days when Ahn would teach Ahee and little Keel her very own language.

Suddenly, the ground where they sat began to tremble and move up and down. It was as though the earth was trying to throw them into the air. There was a tremendous roaring sound that completely blocked out the rumbling of the waterfall. The bouncing up and down continued for what seemed like a long time until the whole group was lying down in fear, and little Ahee and Keel were crying. The thundering got louder at first, and then it faded away. The jungle fell into silence, with the only sound being the boom of the waterfall.

"What happened, Mom?" Aloa was the first to speak.

"I don't know; it is very frightening."

FINDING THE WAY

WHEN THE GROUND had stopped moving and there was no more of the terrible rumbling sound, they could hear the waterfall again. Every dweller in that jungle refuge was stunned. Whether they were hanging from a branch or lying sprawled on the ground, each waited for the next shudder to come. When nothing happened, Klint and Kraat dropped from their perches and peered out onto the grass veld. They were joined by a group of Persh males carrying their defense poles.

As they looked toward the waterfall, they sensed that something had changed but did not know what it was. Gathering their courage, they set off towards the waterfall and the base of the cliff. They looked around to see if there was a herd of giant animals or some monster that would have been able to make the ground move. What could have caused the rumbling that had blocked out the booming of the waterfall? Klint's eyes were drawn back to the cascading water. What he saw made him blink; it amazed him.

He shouted, "Hey, the waterfall is now two waterfalls!" He pointed and turned to Kraat. "Do you see what I see? The cascade has divided in two."

"Yes, you're right. Wow, I wonder what happened," answered Kraat.

As they gazed up at the twin waterfalls, they were joined by Ahn who asked, "What's happening? Why are you shouting?"

"Mom, look, there are now two waterfalls…not one. Something really big must have happened this morning," said Klint.

"Yes, I see; you are right. I wonder what has happened?" she said.

The group stood staring at the waterfalls. They were trying to understand.

Early next morning, Ahn organized Klint, Kraat, young Kreep, and some Persh males into an exploring party to take a closer look at the waterfalls and the cliff. They looked around to make sure it was safe. Carrying their arms, they walked to the base of what was now two waterfalls.

Ahn said, "Let's check the cliff to see if anything is different. Maybe the shape has changed."

The party turned left and proceeded to follow the line of the cliff, keeping close to the undergrowth at its base. They were going toward the place where the young Persh was killed by the boulder.

Suddenly Klint shouted, "Look, the cliff stops ahead, just where the young Light Hair was killed."

"Yes, it's as though the cliff beyond has disappeared," Ahn said, "Let's keep going. We'll see what happened."

They reached the place where the cleft had been and pushed their way through the undergrowth. Where the cleft had been was now a long smooth rock sloping up to the sky. There was no cliff.

"Let's climb to the top to see where it goes," said Kraat.

When they had reached the top, they found themselves looking out over a vast grassland veld. This stretched away to a line of green hills before a white peaked mountain in the far distance. The dark face of a jungle stood to one side.

"This is it!" shouted Ahn in her excitement. "This is the way we need to go. We will find the nest of The White Face."

Klint noticed the dark shapes of some unknown animals in the distance, and he warned, "We may have to deal with some new dangers over there."

Ahn said, "Let's go back to the waterfall now. But this is the way we must go."

The exploring party turned around and retraced their steps down the sloping rock and back to their jungle refuge.

GETTING THINGS READY

THE NEXT SUNRISE Ahn called to her family and all the Kee Persh besides the lookouts. She called them for a gathering out on the grass veld, in front of the first line of trees. Ahn sat in the grass with Klint, Kraat, Kreep, Ahah, Alina, and Ansoa. All her grandchildren were there, Aloa, Krink, Alma, Keep, Ahee, and Keel, three females and three males. Aloa and Alma cuddled Alaha and Kraam, Ahn's great-grandchildren.

The Persh and Cru, the sole remaining survivor of Ahn's ancestral band of Dark Hair Kee Persh, formed a wide semi-circle around them. Two red wolves arrived and sat outside the circle.

Ahn explained her plans, "We have been to a place where the cliff is no more. There is nothing to stop us heading off on our journey to find the nest of The White Face. We will wait until Alaha and Kraam have grown a little," she continued, "The Light Hair males can use the time to practice with their defense poles and cutting stones.

Klint, Kraat, and Kreep will join them to help make up for the lost members.”

“Do we need to bring anything with us?” it was Aloa; she was worried about her new little one.

“Yes,” answered Ahn, “we must gather the leaves, berries, and nuts we will need if we cannot find food. These are important, especially for the little ones. All right, any other questions?”

“Do we need to continue to wear our grass skirts?” asked young Krink.

He didn’t like to wear the same garment as his female kin.

“What! You’re asking me whether you should continue to wear a grass skirt?” shot back Ahn, “The answer is this, I insist that all my offspring, of every generation, continue to wear a grass skirt until the day they die. Do I make myself clear? So, the answer is yes. You had better always wear your grass skirt. If you do not, you will be banished from the family and from the group. Do you understand?”

“Yes, Mom, I understand.”

“When we leave, I would like you two, Aloa and Alma, to keep Bitsi and Kitsi close by. These lovely lady Light Hairs are very helpful around little ones. Then she shouted, “Gruuu..!” a happy Persh word and “Graw,” meaning “go.” Ahn finished, “Thank you, everybody. We will get back to whatever we were doing.”

They all then merged back into the gloom of the jungle.

BACK IN THE QUEST

IT HAD BEEN MANY SEASONS, wet and dry, between the time Ahn had been stopped in her progress by the high cliff - until the earthquake event. Now the recent wet season was truly over, and it was time to set off again to follow her dream.

The journey began in the cool of the morning. Her male children, Klint, Kraat, Kreep, and even grandson Krink, had been called on to take the place of missing male Kee Persh. When the whole group was assembled into the marching column lines, they set off toward the long slope that led to the world beyond the cliff. The column climbed up the long slope and reached the top while the Sun was still rising.

As they reached the high grassland veld, a herd of gazelle was startled and scattered away from them. Away in the distance was a line of tree-covered hills. The dark face of a jungle stood to one side. The column moved to be close to the jungle as its trek began. It was headed for the hills far ahead. Ahn was thinking, 'I'm so happy now that we have been able to leave the waterfall behind and follow my dream.'

As she daydreamed, she was staring past the hairy heads of those in front. Suddenly Ahn was shocked to the core. It was as though a cutting stone had slashed across her mind. Straight ahead was a pride of lions standing among some bushes. The sight of the lions struck a deep wound. A picture of lionesses destroying her family flashed into her memory.

She hissed again and again, "Grek…grek…grek… stop," until the column stopped. Then she repeated, "Grraa…grraa…go, go," as she turned in fear, crashing through the nearby undergrowth and into the jungle.

The column sensed the danger and followed her. They followed her again as she climbed a tree in panic. She sat perched on a branch and thought, 'What has happened? I have lost control. This cannot be.'

Finally, she called out, "Graw…graw…follow me," and began to swing branch by branch, tree by tree, to continue the journey, keeping to the treetops. It was a slow way to travel, but it would be safe.

When Ahn thought they had traveled far beyond the lair of the lions she called out to Klint, "We will go out into the sunlight here."

The whole group swung down to the ground. Fatefully, they had arrived at a rock-strewn clearing surrounded on three sides by tall trees. On the fourth side the landscape fell away to a misty valley.

The Dark Hair New Beings and Kee Persh spread themselves out in the sunlight. Klint made sure that they were safe. Lookouts were put in place around the gathering.

The Sun was getting lower in the sky but the day continued to be bright. Ahn was still shaken by the sight of the lions but she sat high on a rock and looked over the scene. She realized that she must shake off the painful memory and be consoled by the sight of the fruits of her life arrayed before her.

Ahn's Dark Hair children, grandchildren, and great-grandchildren were bathed in sunlight. Klint, Kraat, Kreep and Ahah, Alina and Ansoa were there. All her grandchildren were playing with each other, or with the young Persh. The sight of Aloa and Alma cuddling Alaha and Kraam, her great-grandchildren, was very sweet. She had a feeling of great fulfillment. This feeling covered her pain like a warm flowing liquid. She had a tender memory of Croh.

"Isn't this beautiful?" she said to Klint, who sat below her. "I was shocked to see those animals, the ones that killed my family. The sight touched a painful memory…but I'm fine now."

"You looked so frightened."

Ahn thought, 'I don't think he would understand what I'm talking about. I think I will just have to keep loving what I see before me.'

She told Klint, "I am so happy to be able to love you all."

It was decided that they rest until the next sunup.

As the Sun began to sink behind the trees, Ahn took a last look out over the misty valley. Hanging not very far away was a translucent ball that caught the last rays of the setting Sun. Ahn watched in silence as it hovered for a while. She was still watching as it slowly drifted away and disappeared into the twilight.

OF TORTOISES AND MAMMOTHS

AT SUNRISE, Ahn looked out over the valley. There was no sign of a translucent ball. Fatefully, there was also no sign of lions or other dangerous animals. They gathered into their marching column and resumed their journey. Ahn's three grown sons joined the armed Persh males. Klint headed one line while his younger brothers, Kraat and Kreep, joined the other. The younger males and the females carried anything that needed to be carried. They headed off towards the distant hills.

The going was easy as they tramped down a slope. Then, a strange sight awaited them when they rounded a corner of the jungle. The ground before them sloped down to a sunken gulley, and they had come upon what looked like a long line of bushes of a dark color. As the group got closer these turned out to be not bush but a parade of tortoise shells. A line of tortoises was emerging from the base of a stand of trees on one side and moving to the jungle in the opposite direction. It was as though a stream of tortoise shells was flowing across the valley and disappearing into the jungle.

Klint gave the signal to stop, "Grek…grek…"

The group stopped and spread out to look at the strange scene. As the tortoises were disappearing into the jungle, the whole group looked on in amazement.

But then there was a warning cry by a Kee Persh at the rear, "Greeh…greeh…greeh…"

Ahn whirled around to see a horrifying wall of giant animals coming over the hill behind them. She didn't know what they were, but they were mammoths. Their enormous tusks, which waved before them, glinted in the sunlight.

The mammoths rumbled along, shoulder to shoulder, quickly closing on the group. Ahn looked around in panic. What would they do? She feared for her children and for the Persh. Beyond the moving mass of tortoises was a hill strewn with huge boulders.

Ahn quickly thought out the situation and shouted, "Everyone run for the rocks. Graw…graw…graw! Get beyond the moving shells as fast as you can. Bring the little ones. "Graw…graw!"

No sooner had Ahn shouted than the whole group began to run to the tortoise shells and hop shell by shell towards the boulders. The adults helped the frail and very young. As they reached the rocks, they slid between the massive stones and found protection.

They heard a horrible sound, "Krack…krack…krack."

Mammoth hooves were crushing tortoise shells. The animals were trampling on the tortoises as they closed in on the group. When the first mammoths reached the boulders, their tusks rattled against the stones. Their huge hooves stumbled as they tumbled forward and collapsed.

By now, the Dark Hairs and the Persh were climbing the rock-covered hill to safety. They looked back to see that the mammoths had been stopped in their tracks.

As the hill rose to a blue sky, Krink, and Keel were the first to reach the top. They looked over at what was beyond.

Krink shouted, "Look! Oh, look! There's a river, a big river."

Soon the whole group had reached the top of the hill and could see that there was a wide valley with a river running through it. Grassy banks and dense jungle lined the river on each side.

Ahn made sure that the way looked clear and then she said, "We need to get into formation when we get down to the river bank. We will follow the river. Let's go! Graw… graw…"

When they had reached the river and got in line, they set out along the river bank beside the undergrowth which skirted a jungle.

BY THE RIVERSIDE

THE RIVER FLOWED towards a snow-capped peak far away, beyond a line of hills and a misty valley. As the Sun began to sink and the light began to fade the sky behind them was changing. Dark clouds were billowing and reminding them that the season of the rains would soon be upon them. They did not know that those dark clouds were already full of a rain deluge that was coming their way. It was growing darker, and the air was becoming cool.

They trudged along in waist-high bush and hoped to find a clearing where they could spend the night. Soon large raindrops were falling, and a strong breeze blew.

"Grek…grek…grek…let's stop here," shouted Ahn, "we'll sleep among the bushes, near the jungle."

The group sank down where they were. Nuts and berries began to be passed around. Aloa was feeding her baby, and a Kee Persh mother was feeding her young. The rain became a sizzling downpour with wind gusts swirling the rain into water spouts. There was little to be done except to sit on the ground and wait out the storm. A couple of the Persh began to panic and leaped up, ready to run to the jungle.

"Graak…graak…stay here," shouted Klint, "we need to stay together."

Anh could barely hear her son through the storm. She was holding little Kraam, rocking him back and forth as the little one whined.

"Grraa…grraa..!" one of the Persh shouted in alarm as waves of icy water began swirling around the resting bodies.

The river was overflowing its banks. There was one strong wave after another, and these rushed across the ground where the group huddled. The ground was matted with layers of fallen vegetation and Anh was still clutching little Kraam when the ground beneath her began to shift. Now she and two Persh males were suddenly floating on a raft of branches.

Ahn could feel its movement and cried out, "Klint, oh Klint," in terror.

Klint heard something through the torrential rain but could not make out the sound. There were other cries lost in the storm's roar as Ahn and the Persh were being swept out onto the swollen river. Other parts of the ground started to move.

Klint screamed, "Hang on…hang on."

Persh and Dark Hairs grasped for any bush or stump they could find.

The storm deluge continued throughout the night until, about daybreak, the rain slowly subsided, and the river level began to fall.

As soon as he could see anything beyond his outstretched arm Klint looked around to see what had happened. Those near him were completely drenched by the rain but otherwise seemed to be all right. But there were gaps. Where was his mother? Klint realized in horror that his beloved mother had disappeared. His mind filled with fright, 'Where is she?' He looked at the swollen river flooding by and thought, 'Has Mother been swept away? Is she below the waves?' Klint sank into the mud and began to sob uncontrollably. Ahah realized what had happened and began to cry.

Kreep, her younger brother shouted, "No…no…no… where are Kraat…and Alina…and Aloa…and little Alaha? Where are they?"

Ahah screamed, "Where are Ahee and Krink? …Some of our Light Hairs are missing."

One of the older male Persh stood up to his ankles in the receding water.

He knew what had happened and grunted, "Graw… graw…"

He pointed towards the river and beckoned to Klint. Klint saw him pointing and stopped his sobbing. He understood that the old Persh wanted him to go to the river, that he wanted him to search in the river. Klint tried to compose himself. He realized that he had to take control of the situation; it was up to him to take charge. He called the survivors together on the muddy river bank.

When things had quietened down, he could talk, "Graak…graak…we all need to calm down and think about our situation. I must find my mother and my sisters. A

Voice speaks to Mother to guide her. How could we go on without her?"

Then Kreep asked, "How will we find her? She will probably still be floating down the river."

"I realize how terrible the situation is," said Klint, "but we must make every effort to find Mother and the others. We will set off along the river bank, searching until we find them. Hopefully, they have gotten caught up somewhere on the banks, and we will be able to rescue them."

The group set off along the river in their search. There were the remaining male Persh with Klint and his brother and two nephews. Each carried a defense pole and a cutting stone. As they searched, Klint remembered what his mother always said about The Voice; she spoke about how "…it was always encouraging." She spoke about the time when "She and The Melodious Voice would meet."

Despite the comforting memory, there was a burning sensation of grief in Klint's chest, but he knew that he must focus on the search ahead and ignore the terrible feelings. He hoped that he would be meeting his mother soon. Klint had never been separated from Ahn before.

The Persh were also utterly devoted to Ahn and would do anything to find her. Klint knew that they would help him and bring her to safety. But as they all searched along the banks, the very speed of the river rushing past seemed to sweep away hope. Snakes and other reptiles were floating by. How would Mother survive?

53

THE SEARCH

AHN WAS TERRIFIED in the darkness. She was hurtling along on the surging river and being lashed by a deluge of rain. As she clutched little Kraam to her brest the Persh clung to her arms, one on each side. They seemed to be floating faster and faster.

"Grraa…grraa…hang on…hang on," shouted Anh while the little one cried and cried.

Suddenly there was a thump and grinding sound. The raft they had been riding on had come to rest against a sandbank. Anh rolled onto the sand with little Kraam, and the Persh jumped right behind them.

At dawn, Ahn realized that they had landed on an island in mid-stream. The little island was nothing more than a patch of sand and grass dotted with boulders. She did not know that the island had saved them from being lost on the rocks further downstream. They lay on the grass, glad to be safe, relieved that their terrifying journey had come to an end. It soon dawned on Anh that they were still in great peril. Though they were exhausted and little Kraam and the Persh had fallen asleep, Anh could not.

She began to ask aloud of The Melodious Voice, "What can we do, oh Voice? I know that I am here for a great purpose. I so often hear you inside me and can see the sky above and The White Face. Has my life now come to an end without my purpose being fulfilled?" she cried, "How can this be? Is there no way out? Is there anything you can do to help me?"

Anh was crying, but her cries and sobs were lost in the booming sound of the river. The Persh and little Kraam awoke to Anh's cries and began to whimper softly. Eventually, after Anh had worn herself out and become hoarse, crying for help, she got up with Kraam in her arms, and crawled to the end of the island. Her heart sank with the thought that this was the end of her journey and that she must die of starvation here. She returned to where she had lain on the grass and began to weep thinking, 'When would she hear The Melodious Voice?' She fell into a fitful sleep from exhaustion, lying in a fetal position. Her great-grandson was curled up in her arms.

Ahn was awakened by The Melodious Voice, "…What is happening to my little New Being? How did you get into this situation? Never mind, we cannot allow this to happen to you. This cannot be…"

For once, The Melodious Voice seemed to be concerned.

A DARING RESCUE

Klint and the others came around a bend in the river. The current was not so fast now. Drowned animals and branches of trees did not float by so quickly. Where the river narrowed, they could see there was a low island sitting out on the dark water.

"What are those figures?" Klint thought out loud, "Is that Mother?" Then he shouted, "That is Mother and two Light Hairs."

The rescuers began to run along the river bank to where they would be opposite the island. They were waving and shouting above the roar of the river. Would the Persh hear them? Then one of the two Persh on the island spotted the waving hands. Anh and the Persh began waving to those on the shore.

Tears wanted to well up in Klint's eyes, but his body froze. How would he reach his mother? He stood for a long time, looking toward the island and wondering what to do.

Suddenly, as though inspired, an idea came to him through his anguish.

He shouted to those around him, "We need lengths of vine. Let's go and find them."

Soon he, and the remaining adult Dark Hairs, including Ahah and Kreep, were knotting lengths of vine together to make a long rope. Then they, and the Persh, built a raft of tree branches. These were lashed together with more vine lengths. The raft was moved to the river's edge opposite the island.

A group of adult Persh stood together at the bend in the river and held one end of the long vine rope. Klint grabbed the other end while the Persh held it taught. He stepped onto the raft as it was moved out onto the water. He had a straight tree branch and a sheet of bark at his feet. Letting the rope slide through his hand, Klint pushed out onto the swirling river. The current swung the raft into the flow and, like a pendulum, was carried to the island. As it landed, mother and child and the two Persh were waiting. Ahn held Kraam as she clambered onto the raft beside Klint. The Dark Hair then pushed away from the island while the Persh at the river bend held the rope taut. The raft swung again like a pendulum back to the river bank. Dark Hairs and Persh alike crowded around Anh. Their beloved mother was safe. Klint grabbed the taut rope again and swung back to the island to rescue the two stranded Persh.

When the whole group had gathered safely on the river bank Ahn was surrounded by her Dark Hair family members and the Persh. They all tried to embrace their rescued mother. Klint wept with relief as he hugged her. Big tears welled up and fell down his cheeks.

"Oh Mother…oh Mother…oh Mother," he cried.

He did not have the words to express what he felt. Aaha and Ahn's surviving grandchildren also shed tears of joy as they crowded around. The whole group became a mass of hugging bodies.

While the embracing continued, Ahn looked around and searched all the faces. She had a sudden terrible realization.

She was choking with emotion as she asked, "Where are Kraat and Alina and Aloa and little Alaha? Where are Krink and Ahee? Are some of our Light Hairs missing?"

Ahn's second son, three of her grandchildren and her great-granddaughter Alaha were missing. They had been swept away. Several of the Persh were also missing.

Klint said, "Yes, Mother, you are right. My brother is missing, Alina is missing, Alaha is missing with Aloa, and Ahee and Krink are also missing. They must have floated away like you did."

"Do you think they're safe?" asked Ahah.

"Well, they must be on a raft of branches and twigs," replied Klint, "we will continue until we find them. Hopefully, the missing Light Hairs stayed with them. Graw… graw…let's go!"

Klint pointed to the grassy bank of the river as it skirted the jungle. "We had better continue to follow the river," said Klint, "we'll keep searching. We will not give up hope."

After sitting in the grass to recover from the shock and rest, the group set off to find the missing ones.

A SEARCH OR FOR THE OTHERS

AHN WAS RECOVERING from her ordeal of being swept away. Klint took charge of the search downriver for the missing ones.

He said, "I will go ahead with Kreep. Can you two Light Hairs come with me?"

Klint chose two of the older Persh for the search.

"We will surely find our loved ones," he said.

Leaving Ahn and the other survivors Klint and his group started along the river bank at a trotting pace. There was no time to waste in the search.

First, they had to cross a rocky area, and the river bank had partially collapsed at one place.

Suddenly one of the Persh grunted, "Grraa…Grraa…"

The group stopped dead in their tracks. Not far ahead was a heard of long-horned animals drinking at the river's edge. The four waited in frustration until the herd had retreated back to a clearing in the jungle.

"All right, we can continue now," said Klint.

Further on, they saw large alligators on the river bank. These were pulling the carcass of a dead animal towards the river.

"We will wait until they have gone," said Klint quietly.

The four squatted down to rest where they were. Eventually, when the alligators had disappeared into the river, they were able to resume their search.

It was getting close to sundown when they became aware of a booming sound ahead. They came to a waterfall that stretched all the way to the far bank of the river. Climbing down a rocky incline to look at the waterfall, Klint's heart sank in horror.

"A raft of branches could not have survived this," he said, "Unless we can find the missing ones here, they must be gone. Let's shout their names."

"Alina, Ansoa…Alina, Ansoa..," Klint and Kreep shouted.

The Presh yelled in high-pitched screams. They all shouted and yelled again and again until they were hoarse. By now, it was getting dark. They retreated to perches high up in the trees.

At daybreak, Klint and the group began to retrace their steps toward Ahn and the main group. These had taken shelter overnight, and both groups came together near where Klint had seen the alligators.

When Klint spoke, he began crying, "We have not been able to find Alina, or Ansoa…or the others."

"Now don't cry," said Ahn, "The Melodious Voice and The White Face will have them in their care. The river will lead us closer to the nest of The White Face where we will surely find them."

The group reassembled into shorter marching lines and set off, resuming the search for the nest of The White Face.

56

ESCAPE FROM THE SERENGETI ELEPHANTS

AHN HAD RECOVERED from her ordeal of being swept away to the island. She joined Klint as he trekked along. They had traveled like this on the grassy bank until the Sun was high in the sky. They came to an area of low, dense bush where they had to push their way through. Just then, they spotted, standing straight ahead, a four-legged animal with shiny grey skin and a long nose. It was about the height of a Persh male and was chewing on brush near the edge of the jungle. It didn't notice the intruders but Ahn would not take chances.

She called out, "Grraa.. grraa…" which meant danger.

The group changed course and made a wide detour around the long-nosed beast.

Upon resuming their path, they stayed close to the jungle trees. Then, as they rounded a bend in the river, there appeared five huge dark four-legged animals. Ahn had seen these somewhere before. She had no name for them, but they were Serengeti Elephants. These were the family of the animal they had just passed and were now galloping toward the group.

Ahn cried out, "Grek…grek…stop!"

She grabbed a little one and pushed all the way into the jungle. The whole group followed, with adults helping the young and the frail. The elephants were thundering closer, with their enormous tusks waving out in front. Just as the last Persh had managed to slither behind a tree, the leading elephant crashed into it. Its tusks got tangled in the branches as the second and third ones crashed headlong into the first.

The first elephant trumpeted loudly, "Craaa…!" as it fought to extricate its tusks. It rocked back and forth.

Ahn had dropped off the little one and returned to the face of the jungle. She was just in time to see the first elephant untangle itself and back away. Eventually, the elephants found their baby, and the six trundled off and disappeared into the distance.

"Whew, that was close," said Klint, "We only just made it."

"Yes," replied Ahn, "Let's rest for a while. Then we can move off and follow the river."

She thought, 'We should wait here to give those monsters time to get away.' They waited and relaxed where they thought it was safe. Then they resumed their journey beside the river. A journey nearly badly battered by the Serengeti Elephants.

57

THE METEOR

THE SURVIVORS of the terrible storm continued to follow the bank of the river. They never drifted too far from the closest jungle, but still hoped to find the missing ones. There were occasional rain bursts, when they would need to find shelter. But there was never anything like the storm that had swept Ahn away. When the river reached a gorge, the group would find a way to forge it. Otherwise, they would have to detour all the way around.

They had trekked in along this way until the Sun had passed its peak. Ahn decided that they should stop and eat.

She said, "Klint, I think it's time for us to stop here and eat among those trees. It seems to be safe."

Just as she was about to give the order to stop, a fiery meteor crashed into the trees ahead of them. There was a blinding flash and a huge booming thud. The ground shook beneath their feet, and immediately flames shot up from the jungle edge. The trees and surrounding undergrowth were on fire. Flames began to leap from tree to tree and from bush to bush. The fire was rushing towards the group. In a panic, they turned and ran back the way they had come. The crackling of burning wood filled the air.

Because Anh had been near the head of the column, she was now at the rear. She was now making sure that there were no stragglers, and as she grabbed a toddler, the flames reached her. She felt searing heat behind, and the hair on her back flashed with flame. By running as fast as she could she was able to get over a hill and out of immediate danger. When she had done this, she dropped the little one and began to roll back and forth in the grass. But the damage had been done. Ahn was in excruciating pain, and she cried and sobbed wet tears.

"Oh, Voice, why did this happen to me?" she screeched in pain, "Why me?"

But there was no time to waste. The flames were getting closer.

"Come on, Mother, we must keep going," called Klint.

Ahn fought the pain and scrambled to follow the group as she dragged the little one by the hand. Eventually, they were able to find an old river bed that was bone dry. There were no bushes for the fire to burn.

"We'll have to shelter here until the fire passes," said Klint, "we'd never survive in the open."

They crouched down in a big huddle while the air above them filled with heat and smoke, and the sky was blocked out.

Ahn was still sobbing quietly, lying on her belly. Added to her agony was knowing that the group could see that their mother, their leader, was so fragile. She knew this, though pain overwhelmed her mind.

When she realized that there were no fresh leaves to cool the searing pain, she pleaded, "Spit on my back…spit on my back…"

Aaha and Ansoa, and her granddaughter Alma realized what was happening. They gathered around Ahn and began to spit on the oozing wound. To console their mother, they began to hum the lullaby that Ahn had sung to them when she cuddled them as little ones. "…My little darling, close your eyes and sleep… The song of The White Face is singing over you…" As they repeated this, the Persh began to whine. Then the whole group, the Dark Hairs, and the Persh were wailing. The singing of the lullaby and the wailing continued, rising and falling, until the Sun started to peek through the smoke above.

5 8

SMOLDERING EARTH

By now, the landscape was a smoldering sea of heat. Over a hill, blackened stumps were all that remained of trees while smoke rose to the sky.

Ahn was glad when the cool of evening came as she lay on her belly. It took all night and half of the next day before she fell into a fitful sleep. The Dark Hairs and the adult Kee Persh were gathered around her on the dry river bed. They took it in turns to fan Ahn's back with pieces of dried bark.

Then the cries of a little one reminded them that they were thirsty and hungry. They had to find untouched jungle.

Klint said, "We must search for food, but first, we must get Mother to the river to bathe her wounds."

Klint didn't know how they did it, but somehow they were able to get his mother to the river. On reaching the river, Ahn was gently placed in the cool water and allowed to soak. Then it was time to look for unburnt trees. The group would have loved to roll into the water with Ahn, but hunger drove them on.

Klint said, "The wind was blowing this way, so let's look in the other direction, beyond where the meteor fell."

They gathered into a straggling group as well as they could and trudged in the direction pointed to by Klint. Ahn was helped along by two of the stronger Persh males.

Their path took them across the area where the fire had spread. The ground was still hot but mercifully passible. They skirted the place where the meteor had struck and continued further.

"I see green trees ahead," cried Ahah, "But be careful when we approach."

They had found the trees before any of the group collapsed. They broke ranks and raced to eat. The females made sure that any little one got fed first, and that Ahn had succulent leaves.

The jungle was deathly quiet. Any animals had fled, and the group found abundant leaves, berries, and nuts. They were saved.

As soon as the adult males had eaten, Klint organized them to build a platform and nests. He followed his mother's example by always putting safety first. This time it was to first get a place for her to lay down. Ahn was lifted onto the first completed deck, and Aaha and Ansoa applied the coolest leaves to her back. They knew that these would help her wound. The pain did subside a little but still was so bad that Ahn could not move. She had to ask for food to be brought to her.

When Ahn had been looked after, it was decided that

they would all rest. There were many sore feet and burning eyes.

"Klint, we all need to rest and recover," said Ahah, "Mother will need a lot of time before she can travel."

"All right, we will take refuge here until Mother is ready,"

Because there was no sign of dangerous animals, Klint felt it was safe to climb down the grassy bank to the river.

"If we are all careful, we can visit the river."

That is what they began to do. Taking it in turns, the whole group clambered down to soak blistered feet in the cool water.

59

THE SUFFERING OF THE MOTHER

AHN LAY face down on a new, deck of leaves. The pain of her back was subsiding a little but she sensed it was draining her strength. Ahah and Ansoa were very attentive in putting on cool leaves and making sure she was fed the best food. Caring for their mother was their focus day and night.

Apart from her physical pain and the loss of so many children, the fact that the journey to her goal was interrupted was like an extra wound for Ahn. While she lay on the leaves, her mind would drift away from pain to the happy past. Beginning with the appearance of the glowing beings and the start of her new life, all the happy events would start to play out in her memory. She had done everything that The Melodious Voice had asked for. Joining with Croh had given her the children that she loved so much. Now there were grand-children and her great-grand-children, all beloved of her heart. Happy times were spent high in the treetops talking to The White Face. She remembered the times that the male Light Hairs had lined up on the grassland veld, their defense poles held ready. But she also had frustrating thoughts. When The Melodious Voice said, "…We will meet soon…" did it mean that meeting The White Face would happen soon. 'Why the wait?' she thought, 'If only her children had not gone missing and there had been no fire.' The mother so longed to answer her inspiration to reach the nest of The White Face. Her burns were taking such a long time to heal. She had a sense that she was running out of time.

One sunup, Ahn called to Klint, "We must start our journey again. We must find the missing ones so that I can reach the nest of The White Face while I am still strong."

"…But Mother, you are not well enough right now. I think we should wait until you are much better."

Klint knew that his mother wanted to find her family and reach the goal of her quest, but he didn't think she was ready.

Ahn added, "The rainy season will soon be here, son. We must at least cover some distance before the rain."

"But Mother, you're not ready."

"Son, I am commanding you. We must leave as soon as possible."

Klint chose four healthy males to carry his mother, three Persh and Kreep, Ahn's third son. They made a nest-like bier to carry her. Soon the whole group was ready. They reformed into their previous column lines as closely as possible and set off with Klint in command.

60

THE LOSS OF THE MOTHER

THE RIVER RUSHED over rapids as it wound its way down to a misty valley. The column of Dark Hairs and Kee Persh had been skirting along the river bank not far from the tree line. Apart from Klint, Ahah, and Ansoa, trekking in the column were the other Dark Hairs, Kreep, and Ahn's remaining grandchildren, Keep, Keel, Alma, and little Kraam, her first great-grandson. As the river continued to meander to the valley, Ahn's bier was being carried by three Persh males and Kreep. Ahah and Ansoa took it in turns to walk beside their mother. She was still very weak and the daughters spoke with her to help her cope with her pain. She lay on one side or the other. Her back was healing but still very painful. Klint often checked on his mother to confirm that she was all right. He hadn't thought she was ready for this journey and worried about her burn wounds.

As they trudged along, mist had begun forming on the river and drifting to the banks. Klint became worried that they would not see dangers ahead.

"Grek…grek…stop," he called for a halt.

They would check for the safety of the jungle and stay there until the air was clear. While Klint was checking, a misty cloud was starting to form around the bier carrying Ahn. The mist grew more and more dense until it became a white cloud that completely enveloped the bier. The bier was now invisible, shrouded in white. Ahn had just awakened from a dream. She thought, 'I remember a white cloud like this, this whiteness. It was so long ago, yet I remember…ooooh…' She felt a new sensation. She felt as though her life was leaving her body - as though she was being absorbed into the cloud.

Outside, in the group, there were gasps of disbelief.

"Ohoo…? Where did this cloud come from?" A shocked Ahah spoke first, "Oh no! Where are you, Mother? We can't see you. You're completely hidden."

"What is happening?" Klint had returned to the river bank, "What is happening?"

The four who had been carrying the bier had sunk into the grass. A shocked silence hung over the whole scene. Then, as they watched, the white cloud slowly rose into the air. It floated above the trees and, with increasing speed, zoomed into the sky. There were gasps of amazement; the eyes of every Dark Hair followed until it became a dot among the clouds.

Ahn's bier lay where it had been dropped. Klint knelt in the grass beside his mother. He bent over her and saw that her eyes and mouth were closed. He touched his mother's arm. Under her hair, her skin felt cold. He felt his mother's forehead. It was the same, cold to his touch. 'How have you suddenly grown cold, Mother?' he thought, then realized, to his horror, that his mother was dead. His Mother's life had left her body. Klint froze inside. He began to sob uncontrollably. His sisters and his daughter Alma joined him. The females threw themselves into the grass beside the bier and began to wail loudly. The Dark Hair males, Kreep, Keel, little Kraam, and all the Kee Persh came crowding around and joined in the tears. Klint thought, 'Would they never see their beloved mother alive again?'

The sobbing and wailing went on for a long time.

Then Klint cried out in a loud voice, "Oh, Mother, we will continue your search for the nest of The White Face. We will find your life there. Be safe until we reach you in that nest."

Ahah sobbed, "Oh, Mother, we miss you so much. Wait for us; we are coming to you."

WHAT HAD HAPPENED?

DURING KLINT'S PAIN, he was able to form a question for the mother who was no longer there.

"Oh, Mother," he asked her lifeless body, "was it that we could not find the missing ones that finally led to you leaving us? But we kept following the river. There was nothing else to be done. We are so sad that you couldn't reach the nest of The White Face."

When Klint finally came to his senses, he got up from the grass.

He said, "Let us wrap Mother's body in good bark and carry her to the highest part of the trees. The Voice could come and meet her there."

When they had made a nest in the highest part of the trees, Klint, his brother Kreep, and two of the Kee Persh elders carried Ahn's body to the nest. The bark coffin was tied with lengths of vine so that the wind would not blow it away. Before they climbed down to join the others at the river bank, Kreep looked out through the leaf cover to the hills that lay beyond.

"Oh look! In the distance, beyond the purple hills, there is a green forest that seems to glow. I wonder if that is where Grandma was going."

"Yes, Kreep, I see. Perhaps Mother has only just barely missed her goal. It is so sad," said Klint.

Then, after silently staring at where Ahn's body lay, they returned to the river bank and joined the others. Klint felt a voice speak within him. It was The Melodious Voice, the one his mother often talked about.

The Melodious Voice said, "…We have taken your mother to us now. She is at home with us. She has completed her work…" The Melodious Voice continued, "…You will take her place. We will be able to meet with you soon…"

Klint would continue his mother's quest to find the nest of The White Face.

THE VALLEY

KLINT FELT a great emptiness now that his mother was no longer with them. He thought, 'Perhaps she is now somewhere with the missing members of her family.' He inherited The Melodious Voice that had been speaking to her.

"…We will meet with you soon…" it now said.

These words gave him consolation and the strength to continue. He would journey on in the search for the nest of The White Face.

They reassembled into their lines, resuming the trek, skirting the river and the jungle. The river turned sharply before the foot of a mountain. Klint decided that they should leave the river and head in the direction of the midday Sun. He saw a gap in the jungle and what looked like a valley at the side of the mountain.

He pointed and shouted, "We'll go that way… graw… graw."

They headed towards the valley and reached the first downward slope.

Klint called out, "Grek…grek…stop."

He could see that the valley was deep and dark.

"Don't you think it looks dangerous?" said Ahah, standing at his side.

She had always been the more cautious of the two.

Klint replied, "I can't imagine that the giant animals of the grasslands would live in such a gloomy place. Those animals like sunlight and open spaces. I think we'll be all right."

He called out again, "Graw…graw…we'll keep going. We'll keep going until we get to the other side."

The ground sloped down into the valley. Walking was easy, and the column was sheltered between high cliffs. Though rain clouds were forming in the sky above, Klint was not worried. He saw that one side of the valley was thickly covered with trees. There would be shelter if there was rain.

It was not long before the first raindrops began to fall.

Klint called out, "Graak…find shelter."

He had guessed that there might be some rain. They moved in among the trees but kept heading toward the end of the valley. Though pushing forward through brush, and swerving between tree trunks, slowed their progress, at least they were dry. The only animals were tiny, and they scampered out of the way.

As the group moved forward it began to rain more heavily and became torrential. Big drops fell from above, and water began to flow among the trees and swirl around the trekkers' feet. The water rose and reached the knees of the adults.

A tiny Persh shrieked, "Grruh…!" and slipped below the surface.

As she was being pulled up Ahah realized the danger.

She shouted, "Grrah…climb."

"Climb into the trees," added Klint.

63

THE FLOOD

THE WATER KEPT RISING as the group climbed the trees. The adults carried the weaker ones as they swung up branch by branch, higher and higher. The forest echoed with cries of fear as they clambered to stay above the surge. The Kee Persh were always better climbers than the Dark Hairs and reached the tree tops first. But when branches began to bend and break under their weight, they were the first to drop into the rising waters. They clawed at any twig they could find to stay afloat.

Through the sounds of water sloshing through the highest branches there were cries of "Help…help!" from the smaller Dark Hairs and cries of "Graak…graak!" from the smaller Persh."

When the water broke above the highest leaves and kept rising, there was nothing to cling to. Arms thrashed around on the surface. Dark Hairs and Kee Persh alike grabbed onto each other, but both would sink. The water was now being thrown up into waves by what was becoming a howling gale.

One after the other, heads were disappearing. One by one, they gasped and gurgled into silence. Klint was one of the last to drown. A large bird had landed on his head, and he was pushed under the surface.

The only creatures left struggling in the waves were tiny animals of the forest and, fatefully, one young Dark Hair. This one had managed to cling to a rotting branch and hang on for his life. He bobbed up and down in the choppy waves and sizzling rain. His muffled screams of "Help… help…help!" were lost in the howling wind.

The young Dark Hair was Kraam, the first great-grandson of Ahn. He struggled to survive, clinging to his branch until the wind and rain began to ease, He found a large rock and was able to perch there, shivering in shock.

64

THE SURVIVOR

WHEN THE STORM HAD SUBSIDED, Kraam found himself at the edge of a huge lake that stretched between two cliffs - the sides of the valley. There was no sign of the forest. It was deathly quiet, a quiet sometimes pierced by the shriek of a bird. He hung on a rock throughout the rest of the day and into the next night.

The next sunup, the water had receded and Kraam saw the bodies of Klint and his young cousin Ahee. Two Persh were hanging in the trees. There was no sign of any of the others. Cawing birds hovered above and began to swoop toward him. When he realized that he was totally alone, he climbed to higher ground where he sat down and folded his arms across his knees. He dropped his head and began to cry the tears of his aloneness. 'What will happen to me now?' he thought. He was surrounded by pools of water and nearby the body of a small animal. He was reminded of the watery grave where his family lay.

Then he felt a voice inside, "…You, Kraam, have

survived the waters. Keep going little one…I will see you soon…"

As the Sun rose into the sky, he set off in its direction. He knew of the quest of his great-grandmother to find the nest of The White Face. His only purpose now would be to continue that quest. He would go in the direction where he thought the nest would be. He might find help there. Climbing over fallen tree trunks and skirting deep pools of muddy water he made his way. At sundown, he climbed a tree and found a perch to sleep in.

The following sunrise, after a meal of leaves and berries, he set off again towards the rising Sun. A herd of four-legged animals ran before him and scattered away as he passed. He could see a mountain far away on his right. He would use this as a reference point.

6 5

A STRANGE MEETING

OVER A RISE, Kraam came across a body lying on flattened grass among puddles of water. He saw that it was the body of a Dark Hair wearing a muddy grass skirt. The body lay on its back. 'That's a female,' thought Kraam, 'a female Dark Hair.' The female's eyes were closed as though in sleep - or death. Kraam stood beside the body and began to cry. Great sobs racked his chest. He did not notice that the eyes of the female opened, and her body rolled over on its side.

"What are you doing here? Who are you? You're wearing a grass skirt!" shrieked the female.

Kraam was shocked, stepped back, and stared at the newcomer.

"I'm well…I'm…a Dark Hair, but I've lost all my family. They drowned in the deluge."

"Oh, that's awful," said the female, "I'm also a Dark Hair. I too have lost all my family, my aunt and uncle, my sister, my brother, a cousin, a niece and both of our Light

184

Hair guardians. They were all covered in a terrible river of mud on the other side of that mountain. The whole side of the mountain collapsed under torrential rain. My little baby was swept away."

She pointed to a yellow-colored mountain over her shoulder.

"I couldn't go any further. I thought I might die here from sorrow."

She reached over to embrace Kraam and realized that she was taller than him. He was about the same size as her young niece Alaha.

"Oh, you're the same size as Alaha!" she said.

Kraam felt a flood of relief through his body in her embrace. He stood stunned. There was nothing he could say. He just stared at the stranger and then sat down in a daze.

"I'm so happy you're here. I hope you can help me," said the female. "What do you think we should do?"

Regaining his senses, Kraam said, "I am headed to the nest of The White Face. That was the quest of my great-grandmother, and I will continue her quest."

"Did they call her Ahn, yes? Well…she is my grand-mother. I think she was the first Dark Hair like us," said the female. "Is she gone? We might be the only Dark Hairs left. What is your name?"

"My name is Kraam."

"Oh, your name is pretty. My name is Ahee."

"When I'd lost my family," said Kraam, "I heard a voice inside saying, '…Keep going…I will see you soon… keep going…' just like that."

"Then let's keep going," said Ahee, "I see a tall jungle

over there. Perhaps that is where the nest of The White Face is."

THE DISTANT COUSINS

KRAAM AND AHEE set off across a storm-battered veld to the face of a dark jungle. They were headed to where they thought The White Face might nest. Both carried the weight of a great loss on their shoulders, they cared little about their surroundings. As they entered through the brush, they gave no thought to danger. They gathered leaves and berries to eat and sat down at the base of a tree. They ignored the monkeys chattering in the trees above them as they shared the pain of loss in silence. They nibbled on their leaves and berries.

Silently, a large translucent ball swung through the trees toward them. Out of the corner of her eye, Ahee noticed the movement.

"Ohh…! she exclaimed as she stood upright.

The ball approached and hovered in front of the pair. Ahee could see a tall glowing white figure and a smaller green figure inside. The tall figure began to speak.

"Greetings, Ahee, and Kraam. We are passing through

your time and place and sense in our spirits that you are suffering the great pain of loss. Can we be of assistance in any way?"

"Who…who are you? How do you know our names?" asked Ahee.

"I am Angel Absolin and I am accompanied by Green Angel. As for your names; we have ways of knowing certain things. What has happened here pray tell?"

"Oh, Angel, we have lost all our families, all those close to us. We are filled with sorrow."

"I understand, but be assured, all those you think are lost are safe. Their spirits, thoughts and lives are now in a place of harmony and peace. As for you, be assured, we have the power to make your pathway smooth."

At that, the tall Angel stooped down to the Green Angel and whispered something. The Green Angel stepped out of the globe, spread its wings, and flew away into the trees.

"I do not know what the future holds for you, my dears. For now, peace will come into your lives and the burden of your suffering will be lifted. But I cannot tarry. I have duties to be done. I must bid you farewell."

The translucent ball lifted and moved away. It zig-zagged back and forth among the trees as it disappeared. Ahee, and Kraam, stood stunned, their backs against the tree. They then sat down and thought about what had just happened deciding to continue on the way they'd been going.

"I see a clearing beyond these trees. Let's continue that way," said Kraam. "It looks like that jungle is easier to pass through."

As they strode down into a valley, they were

surrounded by the musical chirping of exotic birds that swooped back and forth. Large animals peered out from between the trunks of trees. Faces with large eyes stared at the couple, but no animal emerged to threaten them. The air was filled with the perfume of a multitude of flowers.

"...Welcome to a garden of peace and tranquility, my little ones..." a melodious voice vibrated through the air.

"Did you hear that voice?" asked Kraam.

"Yes, I did, Kraam...a beautiful voice."

The pair crossed a sunken hollow of green moss to a grassy knoll and sat down to rest. Here they were surrounded by many kinds of fruit trees. Ahee was delighted by the abundance of luscious fruits and she turned to her cousin and said, "Oh, Kraam...thank you for finding me."

AT THE MARS SETTLEMENT

ALEX MCALISTER WAS SCHEDULED to inspect Antenna Array Number 4 at 2200 hours. A dust storm had been continuing for two days, but dust storms were not allowed to interfere with scheduled maintenance. At 2200 hours, he stepped out on to the walkway leading to the antennas. Through the blanket of dust, he could just about see the outline of the first settlement beyond the gantries, and a faint silhouette of the crater lip. Before he began his first inspection, he pulled the Record Tab from his right leg pocket. He again pushed those pesky thoughts about swimming at Largs Bay Beach out of his mind.

One by one, McAlister inspected the antennas. All communication with Earth relied on these working perfectly. Nothing could be missed. A minor ground tremor could put an antenna out of alignment. When the inspections were complete and recorded McAlister headed to Air Lock D and the De-Dust cubicle. When de-dusting was complete, he stepped into the elevator and allowed the door to slide shut.

Just as he said "Forth Level," a flame flashed in front of his visor.

He hit the Emergency Descent button and waited a second for the elevator to descend. Already he could feel fire burning through his compression suit. His lungs would have filled with flame if he hadn't been wearing his helmet. At the fourth level, the door slid open. A Station Safety Officer was already waiting with a fire suppressor which beamed into the elevator stopping the fire. Alex McAlister's life may have been spared.

With his helmet removed, McAlister was hurried to the nearest sick bay. Though in agony, he fought against collapsing on the floor. He stood upright while two nurses carefully cut pieces of his suit away from oozing burns. A doctor had arrived and decided that, because McAlister's burns extended to over 50 percent of his body, he might not survive. Even before the suit was entirely removed, the doctor began treatment. He doused the exposed parts of McAlister's body with a burn-healing ray.

When the entire suit had been removed and emergency treatment had been completed four medical assistants lifted McAlister onto an Air-Cushion gurney. The air cushion would support the patient until healing took place. A nurse hooked him up to body fluid supplies and monitors. The doctor double-checked the patient for signs of life.

Before leaving, he said, "I will have a Christian chaplain come by…goodnight, Nurse Amira."

After a while, a chaplain walked into the sick bay. He

stood by the now comatose patient and read something from a book. Sometime later he left the sick bay.

6 8

THE STRANGE CLOUD

THE MEDICAL TEAMS worked in eight-hour shifts. In the sick bay, the night nurse was sitting and reading a book as she monitored McAlister's condition. While she was reading, she noticed a mist begin to form around her book. The sick bay became full of a mist that then collected around McAlister. His body was completely enveloped in a white cloud. The night nurse was transfixed for a few moments before calling the doctor.

"Doctor Ngolo, there is something strange happening here. The patient has disappeared into a white cloud. I need you to come and look."

It took three minutes for Dr. Ngolo to get to the sick bay. When he stepped inside, he could see the patient's body floating as before.

"Oh, Doctor Ngolo, the cloud has disappeared. I swear it was there - all around the patient."

"Well, aren't you the strange one," said the doctor, "Let's have a look."

There was a pause.

Then he said, "Well, I'll be…" his voice faltered. "The lesions are gone. It's as though there were never any burns. I've never seen anything happen like this. I even thought he might not survive. Let's call the chaplain and get his take."

When the chaplain arrived, he asked, "What's been happening? Doctor Ngolo wants me to look at something. What happened, nurse?"

McAlister was sitting up at the edge of a gurney.

"Well, Reverend Chaudary, my name is Nurse Natalie; I was sitting by the monitors when the bay became full of mist. The mist swirled until it had formed a white cloud around the patient. Mister McAlister had burns to over fifty percent of his body, and we were worried that he might not survive. He was just lying on the Air-Cushion gurney. The cloud remained for perhaps a minute and then disappeared through that wall. It just passed right through the wall," taking a deep breath, she continued, "When Doctor Ngolo came by, he expected to see a patient with severe lesions. When he couldn't find any sign of wounds, he said that he had never seen anything like it. He couldn't understand it. That's when he called for you."

"Good morning, Reverend. Thank you for coming,"

"Oh, you're more than welcome."

"Look, I don't remember a thing. They'd completely knocked me out. …I remember the terrible pain but nothing after that. How do you think I was healed?"

"Was there anything else? Any different feelings?" asked the chaplain.

"Nothing else," said McAlister. "You see, I'm not religious, but it seems to me that it must have been some kind of miracle. …Nurse, are you religious?"

"Not very; what do you think Reverend?"

"Well, I can't make any kind of judgment because I did not see anything. But I'll keep you in my prayers. Is there anything I can get for you? Will I fetch you something from the Cafegharfa?"

"Well, I'm famished, Reverend. A Samosa and a hot Kombucha would be great. Thank you."

When the chaplain returned with the snack, he said, "I've just got another call - but I'll be back in a while."

THE RED PLANET SETTLEMENT

THE NIGHT SHIFT CONTINUED. A naked Alex McAlister still sat at the edge of a gurney. His body showed no signs of any marks or burn wounds.

He was mumbling to himself, "What has happened to me? I feel different…I feel light and peaceful. What a terrible pain I had…they thought I was going to die."

He looked at the night nurse as she looked through some clothes in a vertical closet.

"Nurse Natalie, what do you think happened to me? Have you any idea? I feel completely refreshed."

McAlister glanced at a worktop, "What is that green book over there? Can you pass it to me, please?"

Nurse Natalie stepped away from the closet and passed the book to McAlister.

"It's a Gideon Bible," she said. "Can you put on this robe, Sir? I'll just leave it here on the chair."

McAlister opened the book on his lap. It opened somewhere in the middle, and his eyes drifted to a couple of lines that caught his attention. 'Turn you at my reproof: behold I will pour out my spirit unto you, I will make known my words unto you. Because I have called and ye refused…'

After a pause, he said, "Nurse could you call the chaplain to come back? I want to ask him something?"

Presently, Chaplain Chaudary returned.

He walked over to McAlister and said, "How are you feeling now Alex?"

"Chaplain, I feel amazing. Something incredible has happened to me. When Nurse Natalie fetched me this Bible, something caught my eye. I think it's a proverb. Now I feel that maybe God has done something for me, and I don't know how I could respond."

"Well, Alex, from what Nurse Natalie told me, you may have had what we call a miraculous healing. Let's see if we can make sense out of what you just read."

"Reverend, why are you wearing a black garment under your smock? I thought the doctor asked for a Christian chaplain. …I don't mean to be offensive, but you must be a Muslim or a Hindu. Aren't there any Christian chaplains on Mars?"

"Well, Alex, I am a Christian monk. There are three of us Benedictine monks here on Mars. We form a small community."

"Oh, if you're a monk, you're probably a Roman Catholic. When I was young the Roman Catholic students used to throw rocks at us as we came from school. Before coming here I remember hoping that there wouldn't be any Roman Catholics on the Mars project. How do they expect me to even talk to you? I'm a Protestant." McAlister sounded angry.

"Well, Alex, I'm really very sorry if ever a Catholic has hurt you. By your accent, you sound Scottish. I know there have been problems between Protestants and Catholics in Scotland, and for a very long time - a bad situation indeed. But Alex, I'm trained to be a chaplain for anybody and everybody on Mars. I promise that I will never let my religion enter into any dealings I have with you - not ever. Now, would you like to tell me about your experience?"

"All right, Chaplain, I'll be tolerant as long as you keep everything about the True Faith. But hey, you people don't know anything about the Bible. Isn't that right?"

"No, Alex, that is not right. Actually, the Bible is, as they used to say, our chai and chapati! In our training, we spend many months studying the Bible. Now, why don't we get you some clothes, and you and I can pop over to the Prayer Room and talk about all of this."

Nurse Natalie interrupted, "I just heard what Chaplain Chaudary said, Mister McAlister. I'll get a suit of clothes for you right now."

The night nurse opened a locker and pulled out a suit of rest-wear. She set them down next to the robe.

A REVELATION

"So, let's sit over here," said Chaplain Chaudary, "I'm glad you brought that Bible you were talking about. We can open the page you were looking at. Perhaps you can read me the part that caught your eye?"

"All right then, verse 23…Turn you at my reproof: behold I will pour out my spirit unto you, I will make known my words unto you. Because I have called and ye refused…"

"Well, Alex, it seems to imply that the hearer has been cautioned by our maker. But if he turns to Him, he will receive the knowledge he needs. Does that mean anything to you?"

There was a long pause before McAlister spoke.

"I guess it's as though I had that suffering coming to me as a warning, as though I don't acknowledge God. Am I in danger of losing His guidance in my life…and in my future? What do you think is the best thing for me to do?"

"Well, Alex, do you think you could talk to God in your

own words? Perhaps to apologize for your distance from Him. God is always listening." As Chaplain Chaudary spoke, he handed McAlister a card, "This card has the Lord's Prayer on it. You could begin to say this prayer during the day. Also, you could continue reading the Bible passages that appeal to you. Does all this make sense?"

"Well, yes, it does, Chaplain. I am very thankful for your help. I think you would make an excellent Protestant."

"Thank you for the compliment. I'll tell my superior… Now why don't you stay here in the Prayer Room and think about all that has happened to you and on that proverb," said the chaplain. "Oh, and another thing, which part of Scotland do you come from? If you're going home soon, I'd like to put you in touch with an associate of mine. One that could help you continue your walk with God."

"I'm from the Glasgow area. Do you have a monk there?"

"Yes, we have a monastery in a place called Paisley. Are you nearby?"

"Hey, I actually live in Paisley Old Town, which is just next door."

"What a coincidence! We Benedictines were able to return to Paisley after many centuries, and now we have a monastery. I'll contact Earth and get you the name of one of the monks who would be helpful to you."

"Thank you, Chaplain. That is quite a coincidence."

Chaplain Chaudary got up to leave.

"Right now, I'll leave you to your meditation. We can get together later, and I can give you that monk's contacts."

SHUTTLE FOR HOME

THE FERRY SHUTTLE that connected with the Earth Transporter could accommodate forty travelers. It also carried fuel and supplies for the transporter. McAlister's name was on the latest travel list, so he sent a message to his wife that he was coming home. He also sent a message to Sayyrd Mahmood and the people at Coats Observatory Museum. He had been keeping them updated on his experiences.

When the time came, McAlister was securely strapped into a shockproof pod. The ferry shuttle shot through the Launcher Barrel and out into space. He experienced a slight G Force but nothing like that which he experienced when leaving Earth. As soon as the shuttle had docked below the Earth Transporter the passengers retrieved their belongings and transferred.

The first thing that McAlister did was to locate the facilities where he would spend the journey to Earth. After that, he found a place to sit at a viewing port. It would be

24 hours before the transporter left Mars orbit and there was lots to do on board, especially activities to keep fit. But McAlister just wanted to relax and watch Mars as she rolled by below. He was a little sad that he would probably never see her up close again.

PAISLEY OLD TOWN

JANICE CALLED out to her children, "Alisa and Charles, they've just announced that the transport from Mars has arrived at Pondicherry Space Center. Once Dad has had his medical, he will be on his way. It will be so great to have him home."

"How long will it take for Daddy to get here, Mom?" asked Charles.

"He may be here tomorrow dear. He will let us know. Alisa, can you please pop down to Malik's Vending? Your dad's nice Argyle beer mug broke while I was cleaning. I see that Malik's has almost the same design. I'll give you twenty dirams, which should be enough. …You know where Malik's is? It used to be Joe Sanchez?"

"Yes, I know, Mom, it's on Well Street."

"Can you go with her, Charles? It's safer."

Brother and sister set off to find Well Street. It had been a while since Alisa had gone in that direction. Well Street was in the one part of Paisley Old Town that had not changed.

As they walked, Alisa suddenly said, "Oh, what is that? It's like an angel."

Behind a low fence was a statue of an angel. Without a word to Charles, Alisa skipped across a forecourt and threw her arms around the statue. She hung on for a while as Charles caught up with her.

"That's a statue of an angel," said Charles, "This must be a Roman Catholic church. You know what Dad says about the Catholics?"

"Well, whatever; I've walked by here so many times when I was in Craig Pathshala School and never noticed it. It's wonderful, but nothing like the real thing."

"Yes, I suppose you're right." said her brother.

"The door is partly open. I'm going to take a peek inside,"

"But this is a Roman Catholic chapel," said Charles, "Dad would never allow us near here."

"Well, you stay here. I'm going to take a peek."

Alisa stepped gingerly through the doorway into a lobby. Then she pushed open an inner door and looked around. 'There is another angel,' she thought. 'I'll go and hug that one too.' After clinging to this statue for a while and planting a kiss on the side of its head, she retreated back to Charles with her mind spinning.

"What is it like?"

But Alisa just touched his arm as they walked off to Malik's Vending.

On the way home, Alisa paused silently and stared at the first angel. Her brother stood beside her wondering what was happening. He thought, 'I guess angels are always attractive to girls.'

When they got home, their mother said, "That mug looks fine, Alisa. We'll have a nice Highland Birdie pie and a beer ready to welcome Daddy when he gets home."

73

ARRIVAL AT HOME

THE EASYWAY HIDROPCAB from the Glasgow Drome arrived at Blenheim Court. McAlister's wife and children were ready to greet their dad. It had been thirty months since he left for Mars, and communication between the planets was unreliable.

Alisa was the first to talk as she fell into her father's arms. "Oh, Daddy, welcome home. We missed you so much."

As McAlister wrapped his arms around his wife, the children joined in the hug.

"Alex, we are so glad to have you back. It's so great to have our Daddy home."

The Mars Auxiliary Team Engineer picked up his alamtah bags, and they walked to the apartment. Little Alisa grabbed his hand as they went.

There was an atmosphere of pure joy as they sat around the table eating Highland Birdie pie. McAlister tried to choose the most interesting Mars stories to tell among all that had happened. He did not say anything about his close call with death. That would be just for Janice - and for another time.

74

EARTH BREAKFAST

On his second day at home, back in Paisley Old Town, McAlister slept 'til noon. Janice gave him his first Scottish-style breakfast in thirty months.

"It's great to have an Earth-style breakfast after such a long break. Hey, fresh grapefruit," said their dad, "On Mars, everything is processed; the tastes seem to be added as an afterthought. Also, there is never any bacon, because of the number of Muslims involved in the project. …This coffee is just like I remember, though, Janet. It's got a real coffee-bean taste."

"I'm glad you like it, Alex. As for the bacon, buying pork here is almost impossible. I normally have to go right into Glasgow to find rashers. I was glad to be able to get some to surprise you."

"Very nice dear," he said and, after a pause, "I'm glad everything has been all right since I've been away. This afternoon I'm going to walk over to the Coats Observatory Museum. I'd like them to know that I'm back. I've been sending them reports about what's been happening to me on Mars."

"Oh, Daddy, can I come too? There is a new thing I'd love to show you," said Alisa.

"Certainly, Alisa, let's put on our jackets and head over there now. Please excuse us, Janice. We'll not spend too long."

"No Scottie, you can't come. Sayyed Mahmood doesn't allow doggies in the museum," said Alisa.

When the duo arrived at the museum's public greeting desk, Mahmood was on duty.

"Well, good afternoon, Miss Alisa. I see you've brought back our Mars Al-Masafer to us. How are you, Mister McAlister? It's so good to see you."

"Yes, Sayyed Mahmood. It's great to be back. I am interested to know whether you received my transmissions clearly. I've heard that Sun eruptions interfere with some transmissions from Mars. Sometimes they are scrambled."

"As far as we know, your transmissions have been getting through. We have regular gatherings in the Egtmaa meeting room, where people are invited to come and share the material. The visual images are the favorites. You have a whole group of fans in the area who gobble it all up. Now that you're back, we'll organize a weekend seminar. We would be very happy if you could lead it."

"That's a great idea," said McAlister, "just let me know when."

"Let's go to Sayyed Singh's office. He'll be delighted to see you back in one piece. He might have lots of questions."

Mahmood led the way.

75

BREAKING A TABOO

WHEN MCALISTER and Alisa were saying goodbye to the museum staff, Alisa pulled at her father's sleeve and said, "Can we go a different way home? I want to show you something that you might like."

"All right, we can do that. Adra Sayyeds, please excuse us. Alisa wants to show me something in town."

Father and daughter walked along Well Street to where Alisa had seen the angel statue.

"Daddy, I want to show you something, and I hope you will not be shocked. It's a statue outside a Roman Catholic church that I really like. I wonder what you would think. Is it very bad for me to like it?"

"I don't know, Alisa. Let's go and see."

When they reached the Catholic chapel, Alisa led her father by the hand to the statue of the angel.

She jokingly said, "Mister Angel, this is my Daddy, Mr. Alex."

McAlister played along, "Glad to meet you, Mister Angel. I'm glad that you make my little daughter happy."

"Daddy, I went inside. Do you want to see what it's like? There is another angel."

"Well, all right, Alisa. I'll follow you."

The pair walked into the chapel.

"Look, Daddy, there is the other angel. Isn't he cute?"

"…Certainly is," said her dad as he looked around about him.

McAlister saw that there were rows of seats stretching to the other end of the building.

He said, "Let's sit down here for a while. It seems nice and peaceful. Hopefully we're not trespassing."

Father and daughter sat side by side on a long seat while Alisa stared at the statue of the angel. She moved her head from side to side to get different views. McAlister remembered the Lord's Prayer card in his pocket and took it out.

He began to read silently, "Our Father who art in Heaven…."

They didn't notice that a figure had emerged at the other end of the chapel. As the figure came toward them, McAlister raised his eyes. He thought, 'That's a monk. What's he doing here? Is he real? Oh right, this a Roman Catholic chapel.'

The monk came right up to them and said, "Good day, Sir. Are you Alex McAlister?"

"Aye, that I am."

"They told us you were coming. This your daughter?"

"Yes, she is. Her name is Alisa, and who are you, if you don't mind me asking?"

"I'm Dom Charlie Wong, and it's such pleasure to meet you both. Look, we just about to have afternoon tea. Would you like join us?"

"Yes, of course, we'd love to," said McAlister.

"Just follow me."

Alisa held her Daddy's hand as the trio walked to the other end of the chapel. The Benedictine bowed slightly as they exited there, in single file, through a side door.

The End.

ABOUT THE AUTHOR

The author is an architect and amateur "phenomenologist". He was born and raised in Ireland. Over the years, he has visited 4 continents and several islands. He has a deep interest in the beginnings of the things that shape our world today.

Gerald Patrick Curran currently lives with his wife and soulmate Nida Fe in Washington, District of Columbia, USA.

To contact the author, please use the e-mail: geraldcurran@verizon.net

BIBLIOGRAPHY

Ross, H. (2008). Why The Universe is The Way It Is.
Grand Rapids: Baker Books.

Ross, H. (2017). Improbable Planet.
Grand Rapids: Baker Books.

Friedmann, D. (2011). The Genesis One Code.
New York: Parkeast Press.

Aquilina, M, (2009). Angels of God.
Cincinnati: Servant Books.

Lambert, D, (2016). The Atom of the Universe: The Life and Work of
Georges Lemaitre.
Liszki: CCPress,

Cann, R. L. (1993). Methods in Enzymology, Co-editor Vol. 224.
San Diego: Academic Press, Inc.

www.ingramcontent.com/pod-product-compliance
Lightning Source LLC
Chambersburg PA
CBHW060314310726